WITCHES

&

WEED

CHAPTER 1

Joan's head was spinning. She sat in the passenger seat of her own car, tightly gripping a warm paper bag stuffed with fragrant, foil-wrapped burritos. She chanted to herself, in the privacy of her own skull, "You can't eat the burritos yet. You can't eat the burritos yet. You can't eat the burritos yet."

"You know you're saying that out loud, right?" said Sadie from the driver's seat.

Crap. "I'm really high," said Joan.

She dropped the sack into her lap and twisted to face the back seat so she could tell Brandon and Veronica too. "I'm really high, guys. Are you really high?"

Brandon was engrossed in a close examination of a certain square inch of the tattoo sleeve that adorned his left arm and didn't respond.

Veronica smiled widely and leaned forward, her head right next to Joan's. Veronica's long auburn hair smelled like coconut. "I don't know, but I think I might be. But only if it's not normal to feel all of the feelings in all of my toes. Is it normal to feel all of the feelings in all of my toes?"

"All at once, you mean?" Joan asked. She grabbed a piece of her own honey-blonde ponytail and pulled it toward her nose. It didn't quite reach, but she thought maybe it smelled like strawberry.

"Yeah. All at once. In all the toes. All of them."

Joan giggled. "I don't think that's normal. Maybe one or two toes. But not all of them. Not all at once. That's not normal."

Veronica's smile faded and she nodded solemnly. "Then, yes, I am also really high."

Brandon looked up. "Hey, Joan, can we eat the burritos now?"

Joan turned back to face the front, grabbing the food and lifting it to her face. "Ohmigod, you guys, I have a whole bag of burritos here in my hands!"

"That's wonderful! Can you feel all the feelings in your hands?" Veronica inquired.

"No," said Joan. "I just feel the steamy burrito feelings. Soooooooo waaaaaaaaaaaaaaarm."

Sadie cleared her throat as she turned the car into Joan's long driveway. The three passengers gave her their full attention, Joan lowering the bag back to her lap.

"You guys are adorable," said Sadie. "We're almost there. You'll get your burritos soon enough."

Joan looked out the window as they pulled up to her house, and her heart filled with steamy burrito-like warmth. She loved her house so much, and the three acres it sat on, and her beautiful gardens and teeny little forest and her lab. Oh, and there was her cat, Friday! She was such a beautiful cat and so sweet and happy and fluffy.

Sadie opened the car door and held out a hand. "Yes, Friday is delightful, Joan. Are you coming? I can take the bag."

Sadie was beautiful too. Sadie had been her best friend since kindergarten and she was so full of life all the time.

"Well, thanks, Joanie!" Sadie laughed. "You're my best friend too! The whole talking about me in the third person thing is kind of creeping me out, though, so maybe cut that out."

"I said it out loud again?" Joan handed the bag to Sadie and unbuckled her seatbelt. Sadie tucked the sack into the crook of one arm and extended her other hand again.

Joan was pretty sure she'd never been this high before. Honestly, she wasn't much of a stoner, generally, although she'd smoked a fair amount in her twenties. The only reason she had gotten high that day was because of the curse.

When she was six, Joan and her whole first-grade class had been cursed by their teacher, Mrs. Olsen, making them mute and blind in varying degrees, for the next few days. To everyone's relief, the effects had gradually faded, and most of the adults had dismissed it as mass hysteria. Eventually, most of the kids had too.

But the wording of the curse had contained a clause that implied that it would be back in thirty years, and some of the class, Joan included, had never forgotten that. Joan and a few others had dedicated their lives to lifting the curse. And then, a couple of hours ago, they had encountered their old teacher's daughter, and they'd pissed her off. She had retriggered the curse a few months early.

Joan had figured out that smoking pot made the effects go away. Sadie's symptoms had been the lightest, so Joan had sent her to a cannabis dispensary to get a pre-rolled joint. They'd smoked it, and their symptoms had gone away.

Unfortunately, Mrs. Olsen's daughter, Wendy, had also gotten away, and they had no way of knowing if the results of the herb they'd smoked were permanent. If so, would they stave off whatever might happen when the actual thirty-year mark hit in a few months? If not, was there a way to make it permanent?

They had decided they needed to regroup with the rest of their friends, who were back at Joan's house, and figure it out. And there was the matter of reaching the others in their class, who were presumably also dealing with curse symptoms.

But they also had the munchies, so they'd stopped for burritos on the way. Sadie had been able to get away with only smoking a teensy bit so she'd driven.

Joan grabbed Sadie's still-outstretched hand and heaved herself out of the car, stumbling a little. Sadie steadied her and gave her a gentle push toward the porch, where Brandon and Veronica were already waiting.

Joan watched, captivated, as Brandon took off his black-rimmed glasses and polished them on his plain charcoal t-shirt. He tried to put them back on and missed his face. He tried again, more slowly, and almost poked his eye out. What a dreamboat.

Joan and Brandon had been an on-again-off-again item for the past fifteen years, and recently it had been mostly on. For the past couple of days, it had been very on. And Joan was really hoping that once they wrapped up the whole curse situation, they'd be on-again forever. She'd overheard him making a similar assertion that morning to Veronica.

"Really?" Sadie grabbed Joan's arm. "He said that?"

"Dammit!" Joan sighed. "Okay, I have *got* to stop saying things out loud. What all did I just say?"

"Well," said Sadie, her eyes dancing, "first you gave this weird little recap about the curse, and then about what happened this morning, and then you stared at Brandon for a moment, and then rattled off a brief synopsis of your relationship and *then,* and this is the interesting part, you said that you overheard him tell Veronica that he wanted to be with you forever. Is that true?"

Joan lowered her voice. "I overheard them talking. And she was all, 'You guys should totally be together,' and he was all, 'I agree, but she's so prickly I don't know if she wants that.'"

"And what did you say?"

"I almost fell over, and then pretended I hadn't heard."

"Of course you did." Sadie rolled her eyes.

"Hey," called Veronica from the porch. "Are you guys coming?"

Before Joan could respond, the door opened, and Derek, the incredibly stiff, unbearably put-together, normally-immaculate, predominant-in-his-field neuropsychologist, stood before them, his lab coat askew over a rumpled, half-unbuttoned shirt.

He grinned and tossed his hands into the air. "You're here! I'm so happy to see you! Did you bring food? We're all starving."

CHAPTER 2

Joan scanned the group as they situated themselves around the large rectangular table on her back patio. Sadie and Ed stacked the burritos on the glass top, arranging them by filling: four each of veggie, carne asada, and carnitas.

They'd gotten enough for everyone who would be there. People were missing, though. They'd thought there would be twelve.

Concentrating on keeping her thoughts to herself, Joan bobbed her head as she counted the people around her. There was Sadie, Veronica, and Brandon, of course. And Derek and Ed across the table, and Sadie's eleven-year-old twin children on the other end of the deck, leaning their backs against Veronica's giant dog as they read *The Secret Garden* for their English class. Oh, and Derek. No, she'd already counted him. Plus her. That was eight.

She considered for a moment and decided that it wasn't a weird question.

"Who's missing?" she asked.

Ed sat down across from her, grabbing a veggie burrito as he responded. "Paul was freaking out about missing work. Lily apparently lives close to Paul's office and wanted to go home. Susan didn't want either of them to drive, so she took them. And Beth refuses to smoke pot, so she's laying down on Veronica's bed. She kept pushing it away and whispering about the devil. It was good shit, too – Susan's homegrown. I figure if she doesn't want it, she can stay blind."

"Oh, come on!" Sadie pushed back her chair and bounced to her feet, pacing the deck. "You can't be serious! What hole has she been living in? I know scads of Christians who smoke weed."

Ed shrugged. "She ain't one of them."

A mischievous grin spread across Sadie's face as she pivoted toward the house. "Then again, who says she has to smoke it?"

"Well, that's what seems to have worked for everyone else, sweetie," said Veronica.

"Right. But we should see what else works too. You know, for science." Sadie skipped back into the house, the screen door slamming behind her.

"Why is Beth so obsessed with the devil?" Veronica asked. "Shouldn't she be more interested in doing what's good, instead of not-doing what's bad?"

"I get it," said Derek thoughtfully. "She's been touched by evil, by the curse. Hurt by it. So now she's always on the defense."

The group was silent as they pondered this. Joan's attention was caught by the coo of a nearby bird, and she closed her eyes to hear it better.

She opened them at the sound of Brandon's voice. "Well, okay, now I feel bad for making fun of her so much. That makes sense. We all deal with shit in different ways."

The door opened, and Joan turned around to see Sadie leading a nervous Beth outside.

"Okay," said Sadie, gently guiding Beth forward to the empty seat next to Joan. "Step over the door jamb. Now take two steps to the table. And here's a chair. Doesn't it feel nice to be out in the fresh air?"

Beth nodded silently, groping for the seat. She turned around, lowering herself down. Once seated, she drew her knees to her chest, fumbling to drape her black dress over her legs, and wrapped her arms tightly over her shins. Her shoulders were hunched and her face tilted downward, brows furrowed and lips pinched inward.

Joan suddenly remembered how hungry she was and reached for the last carne asada burrito. She peeled back the shiny foil encasing it and took a huge bite, filling her mouth with the savory goodness.

"Oh, holy crap," she mumbled. "This is the best thing I've ever eaten." She glanced around to make sure everyone was eating, no one missing out on the fantastic phenomenon that was burritos. Everyone except Beth was chowing down, so Joan reached her free hand into the middle of the table to grab one for her.

She seized a silver tube from the veggie pile and was turning to put it into Beth's hands when she heard the clatter of a chair falling to the deck beside her. Startled, Joan dropped both burritos onto the table and swiveled to face the sound.

Beth was now standing, her eyes round, her feet slowly carrying her in a stationary circle.

"Whoa, can you see now?" Joan asked.

"I see everything," Beth said.

"Hey, you can talk too!" said Veronica.

"So many colors." Beth gazed toward the oak tree to her left and then continued her rotation. "All the colors of the world."

"How did you get her to smoke?" asked Brandon.

"She didn't smoke," said Ed. "That woman is clearly under the influence of some powerful edibles."

"I gave her a cookie," admitted Sadie. "I didn't tell her it had weed in it."

"A whole cookie?" said Brandon, his voice tinged with disbelief.

"Yeah…" Sadie bit her lip, staring at Beth. "Maybe I shouldn't have given her the whole thing. I thought she might be suspicious if I only gave her part of a cookie, though."

"She was blind," Veronica pointed out. "She wouldn't even have noticed."

Beth stopped short and her head snapped toward Sadie. "You did what?!"

"Well, you wouldn't listen to reason." She shrugged. "Would you really rather have stayed blind and mute? Now you can see and talk, and doesn't it feel good?"

"You tricked me!"

"Yes, but—"

"No!" Beth wheeled toward the house and staggered over to the door. She flailed at the knob, finally managed to grasp it, and flung the door open. Then she turned around, holding the door open with her foot and reached for the burrito Joan had been about to give her. "This is veggie?"

Joan nodded.

"You're not going to trick me into eating flesh too?"

Joan shook her head.

Beth snatched it up off the table and stormed into the house.

Through the shocked silence came the smacking sounds of someone eating with reckless abandon. Joan turned toward the cacophony and saw Derek scarfing down his second burrito. She watched in horrified fascination as a glob of cheese and salsa fell in slow motion onto the pristine white of his lab coat. He ignored it.

"Damn, these are fucking fantastic," declared Derek. "Where have these things been my whole life?"

CHAPTER 3

Half an hour later, the burritos were eaten, the leftovers stowed in the fridge, and Veronica had checked on Beth to make sure she wasn't going to do anything stupid like try to drive home. Beth still wasn't happy, but she was starting to mellow out and understand that Sadie hadn't meant to be malicious. She was also spending a lot of time lying on her back, identifying interesting patterns in the plaster ceiling above Veronica's bed.

The rest of the group gathered around the now-cleared patio table once more. Joan could feel herself sobering up, and she kept nervously checking in with herself – was her vision starting to blur? Did her throat catch just then because her voice was starting to disappear, or was it just a normal effect of the cool autumn air?

No one said anything for a long moment. Was it because they couldn't?

Finally, Ed spoke up. "Okay, guys. I'm just going to ask. It's been a few hours. Is anyone starting to come down? How is it affecting you?"

Sadie responded, "I feel—"

Joan winced at the rasp in her best friend's normally-clear voice.

Sadie clapped a hand over her mouth, her eyes widening. She lowered her hand and cleared her throat.

She tried again. "I guess— Well, I guess it's obvious. The effects of the pot are wearing off, and now I've got this sexy blues-singer-who's-been-smoking-for-twenty-years voice. I'll be back to a whisper any moment."

Joan squinted across the table where Veronica sat. The woman was definitely fuzzier than she had been a moment ago. Joan opened her mouth to test her voice. "It's blurry," she whispered. "But not as bad as this morning."

A murmur came from the seat to her left, and she strained to hear Brandon. "I can't see at all. And now my voice is—" He broke off.

Joan couldn't see him anymore. Her vision had gone completely white, so she had no idea if he was still trying to talk or if he'd cut himself off.

She heard the sound of a lighter to her right and caught a whiff of that sweet smoke that had suddenly become a fixture in her life. A moment later, the lighter snapped again.

And then someone wrapped her hand carefully around the smooth bowl of a pipe. She put the other end to her lips and waited for the lighter. The heat of it assaulted her face and she quickly inhaled, the acrid smoke hitting her throat hard, burning its way into her lungs.

Joan's vision cleared and she lowered the pipe as she began to cough. Sadie handed her the lighter so she could take another hit. One more puff, and she could see perfectly again. Ed was right – this was good shit.

She passed the pipe to Brandon, molding his fingers around the end and lighting it, just as Sadie had done for her.

As the pipe made its way around the table, Joan pondered the effect that being constantly stoned was going to have on her life. There was no way in hell she was going to be able to keep her job. She could probably still predict the weather, but going on camera like this? Out of the question. She rarely took sick days or vacations, so she had probably a good month of time off saved up before she'd have to go back or be fired.

Joan glanced around at the faces around her. Brandon would be fine. Bartenders could absolutely be stoned. The manager wouldn't like it, but she'd been known to make exceptions for medical needs, provided he was upfront with her.

Ed was already stoned most of the time anyway. He made his living posting ghost-hunting videos online, and smoking weed probably actually helped with that. And Veronica could just make it part of her whole guru thing; the healing properties of cannabis were widely accepted, even among the LA elite she worked with.

Derek and Sadie were completely fucked. In fact, would Derek even be able to return home? The UK had pretty draconian laws prohibiting recreational marijuana, and even their medical program was very restrictive. There was no way he was going to convince a doctor that a curse was an illness.

Veronica, last in the rotation, set the pipe down in the middle of the table. As before, she had to smoke considerably more than the rest of them to banish her curse symptoms.

"Look," said Joan abruptly. "We have to figure this shit out. We can't go around stoned all the time. Half of us will lose our jobs. And honestly, it doesn't really fit my lifestyle."

Ed raised his hand. "Maybe you won't have to. Maybe just smoking a lot will build up an immunity, like it did for me and Susan. I actually haven't been smoking at all since it hit all of you guys. Just to see what happens. And I still feel fine. Slightly annoyed that I'm facing the world sober, but not blind or anything."

Derek shook his head. "No, no, no, no. I can't afford to take the time to find out if that'd work. I've never smoked pot before today. I've got zero immoni... immumi- you know what I'm saying?"

Sadie nodded. "It would take ages for Derek, and for Beth and Veronica too, to build up the kind of tolerance you and Susan have. I'm not much better off as far as tolerance goes, although I guess I don't have to get as stoned so that helps. But I have no more sick days left, and there's no way in hell I'm going to go to work even a little bit high. I could seriously hurt someone, trying to draw their blood in this condition."

"Does that mean you'll get fired?" Joan asked.

"I don't know. I might be able to take unpaid medical leave."

Brandon's phone began a tinkling ringtone, and Joan jumped, startled.

"Oh, crap, it's Jessica," he said. "This will be about the mess we left in the basement of the bar. She'll just be more pissed if I don't answer it."

He hurried away, heading in an uneven zig-zag for the bench under the old oak tree.

Joan's brow furrowed. She had completely forgotten about the shambled mess that was now the storeroom of the bar Brandon worked at.

Wendy, Mrs. Olsen's daughter, who just happened to also be Brandon's ex, had kidnapped him. Joan, Sadie, and Veronica had gone to rescue him and had trapped the witch in a pyramid of fallen shelves and then called the cops to arrest her.

Unfortunately, they had underestimated her, and she had somehow managed to escape, although not before triggering their curse. And now Brandon might get fired simply because of the chaos left behind by a plan that hadn't even worked.

"Dude, we all know that," said Ed. "Who are you even talking to?"

"Was I narrating again?" Joan sighed. "Apparently that's what I do when I'm stoned."

"Well, we need a plan," said Sadie, drumming her hands on the table in front of her. Joan found herself captivated by the *tap-tap-tap* of her crimson fingernails. "We need two plans, actually. We need a plan to get this damn curse lifted once and for all. And we need a plan to find the rest of the class and let them know that all they have to do is smoke a bunch of weed."

"You guys, I just thought of something," interjected Derek, leaning back to stare at the sky.

"What?" Joan swiveled to face him, leaning forward at the intensity in his voice.

"Where the hell is Atlantic City?" he asked.

Ed grinned. "I like stoned Derek."

"It's somewhere on the east coast," said Veronica. "New York? New Jersey? New Hampshire?

"New Vermont," said Brandon.

Veronica shook her head. "No, I think it's New Jersey. Anyway, how are we going to contact everybody? Does anyone even remember all the people who were there?"

"Yeah, actually," said Derek. He sat up in his chair, returning his focus to the table and the task at hand. "I have a complete list of names and I have contact info for most of them."

This announcement was met with stunned silence.

Veronica recovered first. "Well, okay. Wonderful. Problem solved."

"Ummm, not entirely," he admitted. "I do have contact info, but it's been a real bitch to keep it up to date. Also. Um."

"Yes?" said Sadie.

The sheepish expression looked decidedly out of place on Derek's distinguished face. "Six of them have restraining orders on me. And several more have asked me, repeatedly and quite empat- emphort- with lots of swear words, never to contact them again."

CHAPTER 4

Joan tried. She really did. She pressed both palms against her mouth, clenching her jaw, willing herself not to laugh. But it wasn't enough, and as the first giggle escaped with a snort, the floodgates opened wide. Cascades of giggles flowed out of her and the flood spread as Sadie, Veronica, and Ed burst with chortles, snickers, and even a couple of guffaws.

Suddenly, they were joined by an utterly unfamiliar sound. A low, rich belly laugh rang out amongst the rest, and Joan's own laughter died off as she looked around for the source.

It was Derek. His perennially-stern face lit up with a broad grin and his mirth spilled from it in abundance. Joan stared in wonder. What a fantastic sight! What a transcendent sound!

"Derek, you're laughing!" she pointed out, still staring. His teeth were so white she found herself transfixed by his smile.

"I laugh," he protested.

"I've never heard it before," said Sadie, leaning forward.

"I think I did once in high school," said Ed. "Junior year, when the seniors pulled that prank on what's-his-name, the science teacher."

Derek laughed again, his sable eyes sparkling with glee. "Mr. Bauer. I remember that! Everything in the room was upside-down. How could you not laugh?"

"I did laugh." Ed chuckled. "I was just surprised that you did too."

"Maybe I've taken myself a bit too seriously through the years," Derek admitted. His smile faded. "Do you ever think about how you would have been a different person if you had never been cursed?"

"I don't think we would have." Joan spoke slowly and quietly. "I mean, look at the rest of our class. Hell, look at Sadie. Other than the four of us and Beth, everyone got on with their lives. We fixated. Yeah, a few others stayed interested in our work. But they didn't let it take over. Just us. I think I probably would have found something else to obsess over. We're probably just obsessive people."

Sadie tossed an arm around Joan's shoulders and squeezed. "Well, I am glad you did, actually. I never really thought it was coming back. If no one had been working on the problem, and it had returned thirty years later, we'd all be fucked. So thanks, guys, for being complete weirdos!"

"Anytime!" Derek beamed again and lifted a graceful hand, mimicking a toast. "To complete weirdos!"

"Hear, hear!" said Joan, raising her own imaginary champagne glass.

"Where?" asked Veronica.

"No, it's 'hear,' like 'to hear,' not 'here,' like 'we're here'," said Ed.

"What?" Veronica turned her head and squinted at him. "To where?"

"No, no, no, no, no," said Derek. He cupped his ear and leaned toward Veronica. "Hear!"

"Ooooh! I always thought it was 'here.'" She pointed to the ground. "Like where you are. 'Here.'"

Sadie snapped the fingers of her free hand. She started to move her other arm from around Joan's shoulders, but Joan grabbed her hand and held on. "Focus, guys! This is gonna be tough, especially with those of you who have to get super high just to stay curse-free. Ed and I are in charge. We're the most resistant."

"Okay," said Joan. "So, in-charge people, what do we do?"

Sadie and Ed exchanged glances. Ed gestured for her to go ahead.

She leaned back, swinging her legs up onto the table. "Well, like I said before, we need two plans. One for finding a permanent cure, and one for helping the rest of the class in the meantime."

"Let's split up, then," suggested Veronica. "Two groupses. Groupies. Groups. One o' you guys is in charge of one and the other's in charge of two."

"That's a good plan," said Ed. "Derek will have to be in group two, since he's got the contacts."

"Brandon should be in group one, since he knows Wendy best," said Joan. "And I'm in that group too, because no way in hell am I leaving him alone with that kidnapping hussy again. And Veronica has magic shields or something. So she's gotta come with us."

"I think Beth's in touch with a good portion of our old class through church," said Veronica. "She should be in group two."

"Okay," said Ed. "I'll head up group two, and take Derek and Beth. Sadie, you can have Joan, Brandon, and Veronica. How does that sound?"

Sadie nodded. "Perfect."

Joan noticed movement out of the corner of her eye and glanced up to see Brandon returning from his phone call. She tipped her head against Sadie's shoulder. Her eyes softened as she regarded Brandon, her gaze roving from his feet to his wiry torso and then wandering to his forearms. Joan had a major weakness for Brandon's forearms.

She double-checked to make sure she wasn't narrating and then stood to greet him. The blood rushed to her already weed-inflated head and she sat back down with a *thud*.

"Ow," she muttered.

Brandon sat back down in the empty seat beside Joan and she shifted to lean against him instead of Sadie. He put a perfectly proportioned arm around her. Yay — more snuggles.

"Well, that actually worked out perfectly. I still have a job, but Jessica doesn't want to see my 'fucking chaos-creating face' — her words — around her bar for 'at least two fucking weeks' – her words again – to give her a chance to calm down. So I have some time off to deal with this."

"Great!" Sadie hopped to her feet, arms raised in triumph. "You're on Team Deal With This with me!"

"Oh, we're playing teams?" Brandon adjusted his arm and Joan twisted her head to give him a mock glare of protest. He grinned back at her. "Who else is on ours?"

Sadie jumped in place, pointing to each person as she spoke. "We've got Joan Sinclair: scientist! Veronica Grinner: guru and yogi to the stars! Brandon Barber: paranormal expert! And me, your captain, Sadie Fox: less stoned than the rest of you! We will be focusing on finding a cure to the curse, while the other, far inferior team, deals with communication with the rest of the accursed!"

"Cool," said Brandon. "Maybe we should start with Wendy's place."

Joan lifted her head from his shoulder. "You've been there? You know where it is?"

He showed her his phone. "Turns out I don't go to very many new places. It's still in my recent trips on my GPS."

CHAPTER 5

An hour and a half later, Joan, Sadie, Veronica, and Brandon were sitting in Sadie's car outside Wendy's weathered, grey one-story house in Salem.

"There's no car in the driveway," said Joan. "I don't think she's home."

"The house's energy feels empty," agreed Veronica.

"Wait a second," Sadie twisted to peer into the back seat. "If you can tell from the energy that a place is empty, why the hell did we have to go through that whole rigmarole at Brandon's with the cheerleader pyramid?"

"Cheerleader pyramid?" Brandon asked from the front passenger seat. "What the hell are you talking about?"

Veronica shrugged. "It comes and goes."

Brandon swiveled to regard Joan. "Did you perform acts of cheerleading at my apartment?"

"Never you mind," she replied.

He threw up his hands. "Fine. Then I won't tell you if I start playing football."

Joan pondered this for a moment. "Soccer football or regular football?"

"Either."

"I would like to know if you start playing soccer. I bet you'd look awfully cute in those shorts and socks."

"Guys," Sadie interrupted, "we're on a mission here. Veronica, just how sure are you about this energy of the people thing? And is this something you'd be sure about if you weren't stoned?"

"Yes. Like eighty-five percent sure."

"I believe her," said Joan. "You didn't see how she was deflecting Wendy's witchery in the bar basement. It was badass."

"Brandon? What do you think?" Sadie asked.

"Agreed. If Veronica says it's empty, I say we go for it."

"Okay," said Sadie. "Here's the plan, then. One of us goes up first and knocks. If no one answers, we'll break in. We search the place as quickly as possible and then get the fuck out. Anyone have any questions?"

"Yes," said Joan.

After a moment, Sadie said, "Well? What are they?"

Joan ticked off on her fingers as she listed questions. "One: Who has to go up there? Two: How do we break in? Three: What are we looking for?"

"Sadie should knock," said Brandon. "Wendy hasn't met her, so she has the best chance of not getting kidnapped."

"Then again," said Sadie, "Veronica could fight her off if she does answer it, and then we could take her hostage and get some real answers."

"Oh, I like that!" said Joan. "The kidnapper becomes the kidnappee!"

"I don't know," said Brandon doubtfully. "I feel like if it goes south, legally, it won't look great for me if I kidnap my ex-girlfriend. I don't think the whole 'she's a witch and kidnapped me first' defense will go over well. Plus, if we get arrested, we won't be able to toke up, and then we won't be able to talk in court at all."

"Wouldn't the same be true of breaking into her house?" asked Veronica. "Maybe we should come up with another plan."

"No!" Joan smacked her hand on the back of Brandon's seat. The soft cushion didn't give her much of a satisfying sound so she punched the roof of the car too, which hurt more than expected. "Ow!" She cradled her hand against her body and rallied her thoughts. "We have to take action – no more sitting around discussing options. We're here, she's not, let's go and search her house before she comes back! But what, exactly, are we looking for?"

There was a moment of silence while the group pondered. Finally, Veronica ventured, "Books about witchcraft?"

"Yes!" Sadie pointed at Veronica. "What else?"

"Any clues to where Mrs. Olsen is?" Joan said.

"Definitely!"

"Okay, and how do we break in?" asked Joan again.

"Brandon, sweetie, you've been here before," put in Veronica. "Are there any good points of entry?"

"Points of entry?" he repeated. "I was here on a booty call. I was interested in a very different kind of 'point of entry', if you know what I mean."

Joan rolled her eyes at him.

"Does she have a back door?" Sadie asked.

"I mean, everyone *has* a back door. We didn't go out long enough for me to really discuss using it as a point—"

Joan smacked him in the back of the head. "She means the house. Does the house have a back door?"

"Oh. Yeah. She has a little yard and a screened-in porch just off the kitchen."

"Anyone know how to pick locks?" asked Veronica.

"I do," said Sadie.

"Wonderful!"

"You do?" Joan regarded her friend with surprise. "Why?"

"That's not important."

"I think it might be," said Brandon. "Otherwise, we're just going to wonder and wonder and wonder and—"

"Okay! I watched a bunch of videos online a while back. When I was with Sid. Remember Sid? I thought he was cheating on me so I broke into his place when he was on vacation and snooped around. Are you happy?"

"Was he?" asked Veronica.

"Inconclusive."

"I still think he was," said Joan. "He wouldn't let her call him between certain hours. I think he was married and Sadie was the other woman."

"I think he was just a paranoid weirdo who thought the government was listening in on his calls," said Brandon.

"But only at night?" asked Joan.

"Okay, much as I love rehashing all the skeevy guys I've dated, is this really the time or the place?" Sadie glared at Joan. "I'm going up there. I'll ring the bell if there is one, then I'll wait a minute, knock, and if there still isn't an answer in another minute or two, I'll go around back and pick the lock. You guys wait for me to open the front door and then come up. If I don't open it within five minutes of going around the house, then, umm, rescue me, I guess?"

"Good luck, sweetie!" said Veronica, reaching a hand forward to squeeze Sadie's shoulder.

Sadie nodded, took a deep breath, and opened the car door. The others watched as she strode up the walkway, jogged up the three steps, and stood on the front stoop. She took in another deep breath, lifted her hand, and rang the bell.

As they waited for the door to open, Brandon's head popped up over the back of his seat.

"Hey," he said with a smile.

Joan grinned back. "Hey, yourself."

"In all the craziness, I never thanked you for rescuing me from the evil witch."

Joan shrugged modestly. "That's just how I roll. I'd rescue you all over again."

"You're the best, babe."

"Don't call me that."

His smile grew. He folded his arms over the top of the seatback and leaned his cheek on top of them, studying Joan warmly. "You're so pretty. Your hair is like a baby chicken's and your eyes are like . . . blue things. What things are blue?"

"Whales?" she suggested. "Blueberries? The sky?"

"Your eyes are like whales. Definitely whales. Big blue eyes full of magic."

She gazed back at him, wishing they were alone in the car. Sighing, she snuck a look at Veronica, who was ignoring them, staring past Joan, and watching Sadie at the door.

Right. They were on a mission. Joan followed Veronica's example, watching as Sadie shifted awkwardly from foot to foot on the porch.

Sadie squared her shoulders and stepped forward to rap on the door with her knuckles. She moved back again and almost tripped over a potted plant. Recovering her balance, Sadie glanced back at the car and gave them a thumbs up.

Joan returned the gesture and watched her friend as she examined the plant. It looked like some kind of herb with tall green stalks and feathery leaves. Rosemary, maybe? Joan wasn't much of a botanist.

Finally, Sadie looked back at them again and shrugged. She descended the porch steps and disappeared around the side of the house.

Joan leaned back. "Now we wait, I guess."

"Isn't that what we've been doing?" observed Veronica.

"Yes, but now we wait without being able to see what we're waiting for. It's scarier waiting."

"I'm not into scary waiting," said Brandon. "Can't we go around back too?"

"We won't be able to rescue her if we all get caught," Joan pointed out.

"But we're less likely to get captured in the first place if there are more of us," countered Brandon.

"Okay, but—"

Joan heard a rustling sound from the seat beside her and she turned her head. Veronica was chowing down on some kind of vegan energy bar.

She froze, mouth poised to take another bite. "What?"

"Did you bring enough for everybody?"

"Oh. Right." Veronica rummaged in her hip bag (Joan had called it a fanny pack earlier, but Veronica had been most insistent that it was a 'hip bag') and pulled out two more bars. "Almond butter or dark chocolate?"

"Chocolate," said Joan and Brandon together.

"Okay, I'll take the almond," they both said.

They looked at each other. "Surprise me," said Joan, turning back to Veronica.

Veronica closed her eyes, switching the bars from hand to hand a few times and then holding out both hands. Joan grabbed the one closest to her. Chocolate. Excellent. She stuck out her tongue at Brandon and unwrapped the bar, scarfing it down.

As she looked around for a trash bag to put the wrapper in, Joan glanced out the window again and saw Sadie standing in the doorway of the house, waving like a maniac.

"Oh, hey, Sadie's in! Let's go!" She abandoned the packaging in the cup-holder, opened the car door, and dashed up the steps and into the house, pausing just inside the door to look around.

The place was a mess, with books covering every surface and piles of them scattered around the floor, some open, some closed. An altar sat right in the center of the room on a rug adorned with a pentagram. On top of the altar were several crystals, a few jars of dried herbs, and one more book, lying open.

Joan spied a laptop anchoring a blue-and-white checkered tablecloth on a wooden two-seat table next to the side window. She sat down and opened the computer. Password-protected, of course. She tried *1234*. Nope. She typed in *password*. Nope again. She thought for a moment and then tried *Passw0rd*.

Jackpot! She was in!

Wendy's email inbox appeared on the screen. This was almost too easy. She scanned the senders' names, looking for Mrs. Olsen's. She didn't see it, but she clicked on the second email down, a confirmation for a reservation at a hotel.

"You guys, check this out. She's on the run." Without turning around, Joan flailed an arm behind her, beckoning to her companions. "She booked a hotel room for the next three nights in Luzern, Idaho."

Brandon squatted beside her to read the screen, a book tucked under his arm. "Where the hell is that?"

She clicked on the map and zoomed out. "Straight east of here, close to the Idaho-Oregon border."

"Why would she go to Idaho?" asked Veronica.

Joan shrugged. "Who knows? Why would she trigger our curse? I don't have answers for why this crazy witch does anything."

"We should go after her," said Sadie. "Right? She's still our best shot at finding answers and reversing the curse."

"I guess we—" Joan was interrupted by a scratching sound behind her. She twisted in her chair, and her eyes widened as she realized what it was — a key turning in the lock.

CHAPTER 6

oan's heart raced as she leaped to her feet, knocking over the chair and spinning around, floundering for anywhere to hide. She saw Brandon disappear into the next room and bolted after him through the arched doorway and around the corner, out of view from the living room. Sadie followed.

Joan glanced around her new surroundings. The room was probably intended to be a formal dining room, but instead, it was full of cheap, mismatched bookcases arranged in rows like a bookstore or a library. Some of them contained dusty tomes, but many held more jars of herbs and a few displayed various oddities — figurines, strangely shaped stones, taxidermied rodents, a Ouija board. One case was filled with animal skulls – with one shelf full of rounder ones that looked suspiciously human. Joan hoped they were fake, but she was damned if she was going to get close enough to find out.

Suddenly, Joan realized there were only three of them in the room. She nudged Sadie, who was examining a gigantic eyeball suspended in a jar of amber liquid. "Where's Veronica?" she hissed.

Sadie plunked the jar back on its shelf, alarm spreading across her face. She shrugged helplessly and gestured toward the room they had just left, biting her lower lip and raising a questioning eyebrow.

Joan crept to the doorway and peeked around the wooden frame. A short, balding middle-aged white man, clad in dusty tan coveralls, was standing just inside the front door, surveying the living room, his frown echoing the shape of his drooping mustache.

Veronica was nowhere to be seen.

"Unacceptable," the man muttered, pulling a small, ragged yellow notebook out of a voluminous pocket and a short pencil from behind his ear. As he flipped open the notebook and began furiously scribbling, Joan looked around frantically for wherever Veronica could be hiding.

The man embarked on a detailed exploration of the room, inspecting the window blinds, peering behind furniture, bending to study seemingly random spots on the well-worn hardwood floors. Each time he paused, Joan's heart beat faster. Where the hell was Veronica?

Finally, she spotted her crouching underneath the table, peeking out from beneath the fringe of the crooked tablecloth. As the man crouched beside the pentagram rug, his back to the table, Joan waved her arms wildly at Veronica.

Veronica rolled out of her hiding spot and began to creep toward Joan. As the man stood up and wrote on his pad again, Veronica hastily scuttled across the room, sprinting through the doorway just as the man looked up from his notes. He swiveled toward them, his eyes narrowed.

"Hello?" he called. "Ms. Sharp?"

Joan threw her back flat against the wall.

The man's tenor voice floated toward them again. "Are you here, Ms. Sharp? It's me, Mike. Mr. Sutten said you were going out of town. I'm here to do the maintenance you requested."

After a pregnant pause, he muttered. "So what was that noise? She better not have a pet, on top of all this mess."

Brandon gestured toward another doorway and began to make his way stealthily in that direction. Joan nodded and followed the others into the kitchen, where Sadie had left the back door standing open. They hurried through and Joan turned to close it behind her. She peeked back between the ruffled white curtains draping the window in the door and saw Mike enter the room.

Joan ducked down and found herself stooping over another potted herb. This one was immediately recognizable, and she scooped up the large plastic pot, lugging it in both hands as she staggered after her friends, the five-pointed leaves at the top of the bush brushing against her chin.

As they rounded the corner toward the front of the house, the back door opened and Mike's astonished face poked out.

"Run!" she called out, speeding up as best she could, burdened as she was.

As they raced back around the house, she heard Mike's disgruntled voice yell after them, "Come back here!" And then, "Eh, what do I care? I'm not the police."

She slowed down, taking care not to drop the plant she carried as she walked back to the car.

"What are you doing?" cried Sadie. "Hurry up!"

"He's not chasing us," said Joan.

The front door of the house opened and Mike came barreling out.

"Gotcha!" he bellowed. "Lulled you into a false sense of security, I did, and then—"

Joan dropped the pot plant, dashed the last few steps to the car, and flung herself in through the open back door. Before she even had it closed all the way, Sadie screeched out into the road and away.

Joan managed to slam the door shut and buckle herself in. She glanced back and saw Mike shaking a fist at them from the sidewalk.

"Did anyone get anything at all while we were there?" asked Veronica. "Besides the Idaho hotel thing?"

Brandon held up a brown leather-bound book. It was about two inches thick and had an intricate golden drawing of a tree on the front in a Celtic-knot style. "I got the book that was open on her altar. It seems like it probably has whatever she was working on right before she left, right? It's bound to be related to our curse!"

Joan frowned. "Didn't she have the spell on her tablet? That's what she was reading at the bar when she kidnapped you."

Brandon shrugged. "Maybe she took a picture of the page she needed. If nothing else, this has got to be a better resource about actual witchcraft than we've ever seen before."

"That's true," admitted Joan.

Brandon opened the book and peered at the first page.

Joan unbuckled herself and scooted into the middle seat. Leaning against Brandon's shoulder, she studied the volume. The pages were made of thick parchment and on the first one was a hand-written list.

"What is this?" said Brandon. "It looks like just a list of names."

"They're all in different handwriting," Joan pointed out. "Is it the owners of the book? You know, like how people used to hand down Bibles through their families and they'd write down the names of all the kids they had." She pointed to the two names at the end. "Look! Marian Olsen and Wendy Sharp."

Brandon whistled as he ran a finger slowly down the list. "There's got to be about twenty names here. If these are all generations of witches, and you figure at least twenty years between them . . . that's two thousand years of owners! Is that right? That can't be right."

"They might not be one generation each," said Veronica. "Maybe a few of them had more than one kid."

Joan scanned the top of the list; it began with some very old-fashioned names — Helewys, Guinevere, Maerwyn. "I don't think anyone's been named 'Cedany' for about a thousand years."

"This book has got to be ancient," said Brandon. "Maybe we should be wearing gloves."

Joan shook her head. "No, it's a working spellbook. If it was going to fall apart any minute, she wouldn't have it out and open in her living room. It would be in a climate-controlled display case somewhere."

"Oh!" said Veronica. "I bet it's got a protection spell on it!"

Brandon turned to the next page. The cursive was clear and readable — but not in English.

"What language is this?" asked Joan.

"It looks like German, maybe?" guessed Brandon with a shrug that nudged his elbow into Joan's side.

She shifted her position and reached over to flip over another leaf. "Another hand-written page. This one looks like French. I took French in high school, but it's been a while." She stared at the title, unpacking knowledge long-forgotten. "It's either about a lumberjack . . . or a . . . round cover?"

"How do you remember the word for 'lumberjack?'" Brandon cocked his head at her, eyes narrowed.

"We had to write a story senior year. Mine was about a lumberjack and a mermaid and they went shopping. I got an A."

"Okay, so what's 'mermaid?'" he demanded.

Joan thought for a moment. "I don't remember that one."

"Just 'lumberjack?'"

"I guess so. Is this relevant?" She frowned at him.

"It is if you're going to be our translator," Brandon retorted.

Sadie cleared her throat. "Back to the book, guys? Is page two written in the same handwriting as page one?"

Joan switched back and forth between the pages a couple of times, examining the lettering. "I think it is. Why would one person be writing in two languages?"

"For added security, maybe," suggested Brandon. "But then why not just set a magical booby trap so no one except you and your kids can read it?"

Veronica tried to speak up, but only a whisper emerged. "Maybe they— Oh, crap. That snuck up on me."

She rummaged in her bag and pulled out the pipe and pill-bottle full of green buds that Ed had sent along with them to keep up their THC levels. She opened the bottle and pulled out a vegetal orb, holding the pipe in one hand and the bud in the other. She turned her head toward the back seat and squinted at them, uncertainty written across her visage.

"Do you guys know how this works?" she whispered.

Joan shook her head. "On the rare occasion I smoke, I just get prerolls from the dispensary." Her voice was starting to sound hoarse too.

"Give it here." Brandon gently relieved Veronica of her smoking implements. He looked around and found a pull-out ashtray on the back of the center console. Opening it, he tapped the bowl on the edge, emptying it out. Then he tucked the bud into it, packing it in carefully. He handed it back to Veronica. "Do you have a lighter?"

Her lips moved but no sound emerged, and her eyes unfocused.

"Oh, crap," said Joan, then clapped a hand over her mouth at the grating croak her voice had become. Her sight blurred and she felt the car slowing as Sadie pulled over to the side of the road.

The pipe made its rounds and a few minutes later, they were all clear-eyed, clear-voiced, and muddle-headed once again.

CHAPTER 7

The sun had set by the time Sadie pulled into Joan's driveway again, and Joan's energy was at dangerously low levels. It had been a long day — starting with the discovery of Veronica meditating naked on her lawn, then dealing with Brandon's kidnapping, closely followed by the manifestation of the curse, then the sort-of lifting of the curse. That was all before lunch. And the afternoon had been spent breaking and entering while doing drugs.

To say this was a departure from her norm was like saying that Beth was *kind of* religious.

The car rolled to a stop and Joan wearily pushed open the door. She swung her legs out onto the gravel and sat for a moment, waiting for the world to stop sloshing around.

A sudden scream rent the air and Joan slowly raised her head. It sounded like Veronica. Her surroundings were still gyrating like a drunk sorority party — not just one or two girls, but the whole shindig. She closed her eyes and forced herself to her feet.

She cracked one eyelid and found that everything seemed to have settled into its usual stationary formation. Relieved, she slogged up the driveway and clomped up her front porch steps. She opened the door to her house and saw Veronica hugging a smallish, unfamiliar person whose face she couldn't see.

Joan's interest in this situation was short-lived. As she caught a whiff of a heavenly aroma, she perked up, her spine elongating and her head swiveling toward the kitchen.

"Do I smell Chinese food?" she asked. "What glorious angel took it upon themselves to bring Chinese food into my home?" She lifted a hand into the air. "I shall bestow upon you the greatest honor of this land: the absolute highest of high-fives."

Veronica turned, her face split by a gigantic smile. "It's Finn! My Finn came for me and brought us Chinese food!"

Joan raised an eyebrow. "Really? Your partner? Brought Chinese food? You told me when you arrived here that Chinese food would be, and I quote, 'unacceptable.'"

Finn's lips twitched. "I stopped to get her some Indian food, but I figured the rest of you were probably normal, and there was a Chinese place next door. I was hoping it would help you to not be pissed at me for just showing up out of the blue." They gestured to the kitchen. "There's General Tso's and orange chicken and beef with broccoli and lo mein and fried rice and an appetizer sampler."

"You're officially my hero." Joan rushed toward the kitchen, stopping in the doorway to survey the table crammed with open cartons, a cloud of fragrant steam rising toward the ceiling.

Sadie and Brandon were already busily piling a little from each box onto their plates.

Joan turned around and held up her hand again, palm out. "High five. Well-earned."

Finn grinned and smacked their hand against hers. Finn was short, slender, and gender-neutral. They had short, spiky hair, which was dyed pale blue, and wore skinny jeans and a loose grey t-shirt that read *CREW* in black letters. "Pleased to be of service. When my princess texted me this morning about the curse, I couldn't stop myself from coming to be with her. I jumped into my car and just drove straight up here."

Veronica slipped between Joan and Finn and grabbed a plate from a stack sitting on the counter. Finn gasped as Veronica plopped a spoonful of General Tso's chicken onto her dish. "Princess, what are you doing?"

"I'm having some dinner. I'm starving, and this stuff looks amazing." She held the plate up to eye-level, examining the glaze-covered poultry. "It's so shiny."

"You know that's meat, though, right? And that sauce is full of sugar." Finn's blond eyebrows furrowed. "Your daal is over there on the counter."

Veronica nodded. "Yeah, I saw it. I'm gonna eat that too, don't you worry. What's in these dumplings? I don't care. I'm having one." She popped two potstickers onto her plate.

Laughter bubbled out of Joan. "She didn't tell you what the antidote for our curse is, did she?"

Finn shook their head. "No, why?"

"We're all stoned to the fucking gills. Your pristine health goddess over there has the munchies, and she doesn't give a damn what she's putting into that sacred body of hers."

Finn's eyes widened. "I'm sorry if this sounds unfeeling, but this is the best day of my life. I've been trying to get her to eat junk food with me for years."

Sadie's hazel eyes danced as she unwrapped a set of chopsticks and rubbed them together. "Well, thank goodness for you, Finn! I've been trying to find a bright side to look at all day."

"Where's everyone else?" asked Joan.

Finn nodded toward the back door. "Derek suggested we eat out in the lab — I guess the table is bigger."

Silence filled the kitchen as Joan, Sadie, Brandon, and Veronica all stopped what they were doing and stared at Finn.

Finn looked nervous. "What?"

Joan found her voice. "*Derek* said that? *Derek* suggested that we *sit at my lab table* and *eat food* in a *science lab*?"

Finn shrugged. "Yeah. Why?"

Sadie shook her head. "No reason. Our world just turned upside-down, is all. Veronica is eating junk food and Derek is behaving like an irresponsible teenager. I better go check on my kids and make sure they haven't been corrupted by it all." She sauntered outside and Joan and Brandon followed her to the lab. Joan balanced her plate in one hand as she chowed down on a pork-and-veggie eggroll in the other.

The lab window emanated a cozy glow and the sounds of laughter spilled out. At least everyone was getting along better now with the herbal intervention. Joan wondered if Beth was in there too. She tried to do some mental calculations to discern if the cookie would have worn off yet, but math wasn't happening today.

Sadie opened the door and was immediately accosted by her children, who pushed her back out into the yard, Marlon taking her plate and giving her a one-armed hug as Becca wrapped both arms around her mother and dragged her around, shouting, "Mama! You're back!"

Joan narrowly avoided the bulldozing trio as they careened around the lawn, but tripped slightly over the square of concrete that guarded the lab door. She dropped the egg roll onto her plate, watching helplessly as the dish teetered in slow motion.

Just in time, Brandon reached out with his own free hand and steadied the plate, stepping up beside her and bracing her side against his hip.

"You okay?" he asked with a grin.

She stared at him, wide-eyed. "You saved me."

"I mean, I think it was mostly your dinner that was in danger," he said.

"No." She shook her head solemnly. "If my orange chicken had gone away, I would have been too sad. I wouldn't have made it." She stabilized the plate in her hand and marched into the lab, heading straight for an empty stool at the table.

Joan set her plate down and picked up her chopsticks. She was vaguely aware of a greeting from Ed and barely noticed when Brandon sat down beside her. With single-minded intensity, she worked her way through the food on her plate, savoring the sweet and salty goodness of it.

Finally, her plate was empty. She sighed blissfully and looked up.

The room was quiet as everyone gaped at her.

"What?" she asked. Her eyes darted around the table. Ed, Derek, and Beth sat along the opposite side. Brandon was next to her and Sadie on the other side of him. There were three empty seats down at the end. Near the door, Becca and Marlon were doing homework, watched over by a lounging Willow.

Brandon took her hand, his thumb moving in small, warm circles on her skin. "You have a way about you when you get into a groove, babe, that's all."

"Don't call me that," she said automatically.

Derek, who sat directly across from her, cleared his throat. He must have changed his lab coat, because it was now clean, although once again decidedly rumpled. The sleeves were rolled up and the buttons were off-kilter. "Now that we've eaten, shall we compare notes?"

Joan looked around again. "Where are Veronica and Finn?"

"Still reuniting, I would guess." Sadie wiggled her eyebrows suggestively.

Joan couldn't help but notice Beth's lips tighten at this. Still judgy, even on edibles, apparently.

Joan rolled her eyes but said nothing. Instead, she turned her attention to Ed, who was speaking up.

"We've called most of the people on the list, but only actually spoken to three. Michelle Smith, Jason Iverson, and Patrick Mason."

Joan frowned. "Patrick who? I don't remember him."

Ed shrugged. "I guess he transferred in like second grade? Honestly, I'm really impressed with the extent of Derek's list — I don't remember half the people on it."

"How many people are there?" Sadie asked, stepping on the rungs of her stool and leaning her entire torso all the way over the table to peer at the page in the middle.

Brandon leaned against Joan to evade Sadie's elbow, and she snuggled against him, crossing her free hand across her body to run it up and down his forearm. Mmm.

"Thirty-one," said Derek. "Everyone who was in our first-grade class, except for Mary Beth Miller, who was sick that day."

"Huh. I don't remember her either," said Joan.

"She moved away," said Derek.

"How did the people you talked to respond?" asked Brandon. He pulled the list toward him, situating it between himself and Sadie so they could both scan it.

Sadie picked it up, jumping to her feet and pacing around the table as she examined it.

Brandon and Joan exchanged a wry grin.

"Well, only Jason could actually talk to us. Michelle was whispering, but honestly, I couldn't really understand her," Ed replied. "We told her to toke up and give us a call afterward and we'd answer her questions. Haven't heard back, but that was only half an hour ago. Jason was in better shape; I guess he smokes for his headaches. We told him to just light up if he finds himself with any symptoms or whatever."

"And Patrick?" Sadie paused in her rambling, looking up from the page.

Derek shrugged. "It seemed like someone answered. So we talked to him — told him what was what, waited for a response, and then it sounded like he hung up. We figured it had to be him unable to talk."

Beth finally spoke, her voice low and sad. "We left messages for everyone else. I hope everyone will be okay."

Derek reached out and rested his hand on Beth's arm.

Joan studied Beth's face. Her eyes were red and puffy, her cheeks mottled. She had clearly been crying. "How are you holding up, Beth?" she asked. "I know it must be hard for you to call people and ask them to do something you didn't want to do yourself."

Beth ducked her head, staring at her hands, folded on the table. "Thank you. It has been difficult." She turned to Sadie, who was still standing in one spot, but slowly moving from flat feet to tiptoes and back again, over and over.

"Sadie, I owe you an apology. I still wish you had gone about it differently. But I'm sorry I was so angry with you for dosing me. You were right — I was being stubborn and irrational."

Sadie beamed and skipped around the table to plop herself in the empty stool beside Beth. She tipped herself over, wrapping an arm around Beth's shoulders and giving her a squeeze. "Oh, honey, I'm the one who should be sorry! I should have taken the time to persuade you, instead of just handing you a cookie. And I definitely should have broken it in half! I hope you didn't trip too hard."

Beth smiled weakly, her body tensing uncomfortably in the embrace. "I have no frame of reference, but I think I might have tripped pretty hard, actually. It wore off, and Ed was kind enough to give me a lollipop, which has been more manageable. I just gave it a couple of licks and was good to go."

Sadie dropped her arm. She caught Joan's eye and raised her eyebrows, her eyes moving meaningfully toward Derek's hand, still situated just south of Beth's elbow.

Joan rolled her eyes and shook her head. Sadie just couldn't stop matchmaking. Couldn't someone just comfort a friend without being overanalyzed?

"So what's the scoop with you guys?" Ed asked. "Did you find anything at Wendy's place?"

"Yes! I didn't want to get food on this; it seems pretty important." Brandon walked over to the card table beside the door, where he had stashed the book. He brought it back to the lab table and carefully set it down in the middle, facing the three who hadn't seen it. They leaned forward to take a look.

He opened it to the first page. It was now totally empty.

CHAPTER 8

Ed, Derek, and Beth frowned at the book and then at Brandon. Ed reached out and turned the page, revealing another blank sheet where the German spell had been.

Derek picked it up and flipped through it. "This book is blank. What's so important about it?"

Joan opened her mouth and then snapped it shut again.

Sadie leaned over and grabbed the book from Derek's unresisting hands, scanning the pages herself. She held it up for Joan and Brandon to see. "Where did the names go? The spells? What is going on here?"

"Names?" asked Ed.

"Spells?" Beth clutched her cross pendant.

Joan found her voice. "This book was not empty in the car. The first page had a list of names. Like twenty names, ending with Mrs. Olsen and Wendy."

Brandon nodded. "And then the next page had a spell in German and the next one was in French. Something about a lumberjack."

"A lumberjack?" Ed raised an eyebrow. "Who the hell knows the word for lumberjack in French?"

"Joan does," said Sadie.

"Why?"

Derek interrupted. "I hate to be 'that guy', but let's really try to focus here."

"What are you talking about?" Sadie demanded. "You love being that guy."

He thought for a moment. "Good point. So, let's focus! In this state, I guess this book won't help us. Did you guys get anything else?"

"We also saw an email confirming a reservation at a hotel in Luzern, Idaho for the next few days," said Joan.

"We have to go after her!" Derek leaped to his feet, his stool clattering to the floor.

Joan jumped, startled, staring at Derek as he swayed dizzily from the sudden movement.

"Oh, I wish I hadn't done that," he murmured. He shook his head and seemed to recover. "But seriously, you guys, we gotta go to Idaho! That's our best lead."

Sadie stood and picked up Derek's stool, setting it upright. "I can't go gallivanting off to Idaho." She flung her arm in a wide gesture toward the door. "My kids have had their lives disrupted enough the past couple of days already."

"We don't all have to go," said Brandon. "We wouldn't all fit in a car anyway."

Derek resumed his seat, nodding thoughtfully. "You're right. I got carried away. Honestly, I'm not sure how much use I'd be hunting down and catching a witch. I better stay here and continue the outreach."

"Me too," said Beth.

Sadie gave Joan another knowing look, taking her seat again and leaning her chin on her hands.

"Well," said Joan, ignoring Sadie. "Veronica definitely has to go. She's got that defensive mojo. And Brandon and I are the most knowledgeable about witchcraft."

"Wicca, though," said Brandon. "Not witchcraft. I don't think Wicca is really what we're dealing with here."

"Well, no one knows about the witchcraft," Joan pointed out. "So we're the closest to experts."

"I don't look it, but I'm good in a fight," interjected Ed.

"Sounds like we've got a team," said Brandon. "The four of us will brave the wilds of Idaho in search of the wicked witch!"

The door opened and Veronica and Finn entered, hand in hand. Joan waved them over and Veronica led Finn to the empty stools at the far end of the lab table. "Have you guys solved it all yet?" she asked.

"We have a plan!" said Joan. "We're splitting up and you're on Team Track Down Wendy in Idaho."

"Wonderful! How about a snappier name, though?"

"Team Witchfinder?" suggested Sadie.

"Perfect!" Veronica smiled. "And who is on Team Witchfinder?"

Joan pointed her way around the table. "Me, you, Brandon, Ed."

Veronica frowned. "And Finn."

There was an awkward pause. Veronica narrowed her eyes, glaring around the table. "And Finn," she repeated, slowly and deliberately.

Joan glanced at Finn, who stared down at their lap. They looked timid, small, and completely helpless. It seemed like they would just be a liability on this trip.

"I could drive," Finn offered, glancing up. "You guys have to keep smoking, right? You'll need someone sober."

"I can stay sober," Ed pointed out. "I haven't smoked at all today, and I'm fine. I think I have immunity now."

"You think," said Veronica. "That could change. Plus, even if you can stay sober, do you really want to?"

"Not really," Ed admitted. "I'm not used to this. It feels weird."

"So it's settled, then." Veronica crossed her arms. "Finn will come along and be our driver. Otherwise, I stay here with them, and you miss out on my shielding ability."

Beth spoke up, her expression puzzled. "Why not just let them go? Veronica's right; you should have a driver, and we have no idea if Ed's immunity will go away. Or if Wendy can make the curse worse. She probably has no power over Finn. Or at least less power."

Joan cocked her head, studying Beth in surprise.

"Thank you, Beth," said Veronica, with a satisfied smile. "That settles it. And now, if you'll excuse us, we're going to turn in. It's been a long day."

Veronica and Finn stood and exited the lab again, Finn glancing nervously over their shoulder on the way out the door.

Sadie threw her arm around Beth's shoulder once more. "Good for you, Beth! No offense, but I thought you'd be a bit of a creep about Finn."

Beth sighed. "I'm not that kind of Christian. I don't approve of Veronica and Finn living in sin. I think they should get married, and for that matter, I think the same about Joan and Brandon if you're going to engage in carnal activity. But Jesus never said anything about people not being gay or transgender or anything like that. It's none of my business. People should be true to themselves."

Joan smiled warmly. "You're not the worst, Beth."

CHAPTER 9

Joan woke up the next morning, panicking when she opened her eyes to white fuzz. Her anxiety receded after a moment as she remembered the events of the previous day. She fumbled on her bedside table for the bowl Brandon had packed for her the night before. They'd been lucky that Ed had come so prepared — he'd unloaded two pipes, a case of rolling papers, and a whimsical betentacled, octopus-shaped bong from his trunk, along with an old Danish butter cookie tin full of weed. It was the first time Joan had seen those tins used for anything besides sewing supplies.

Each member of the group had been able to prepare a smoking apparatus for the morning, and Beth was still slowly working her way through the lollipop, carefully stowing it in a sandwich bag between uses.

Sadie had gone home, reassuring Joan that she would stop at a dispensary and stock up on her way. She had also taken Veronica and Finn's dog, Willow, as Derek had professed himself canine-incompetent.

Derek and Beth would be staying at Joan's house, holding down the fort and continuing to reach out to the others, while the rest of them chased down Wendy. Sadie, of course, was convinced that they would be madly in love within a day and a half. Joan just hoped they'd remember to feed her cat.

She lit up and took a couple of hits — just enough to chase away the blizzard obscuring her vision, but not so much that she felt super stoned. It had only been one day, but she was already getting good at judging how much she needed without going overboard.

It's funny how quickly one adapted to new situations, however absurd.

As her eyes cleared, she glanced at Brandon beside her, still asleep on his stomach, one bare arm flung carelessly over the pillow, the other disappearing under the comforter. Joan admired his shapely forearm for a moment and then reached out and nudged him awake.

Brandon turned his head, not opening his eyes. He was a slow waker-upper, although he was also an early riser and usually up before her. He must have been exhausted, what with being kidnapped and everything. He had been zonked out by the time she'd come to bed last night after she'd finished cleaning up the dinner dishes.

"Wake and bake?" she offered.

"Yes, please," he whispered. Brandon sat up, eyes still closed — he wouldn't be able to see anything anyway, so Joan supposed that was practical.

She guided the relevant end of the pipe to his lips and lit it for him. As he inhaled and coughed, Friday jumped in through the window and up onto the bed. Joan smiled and scratched the calico cat's neck, luxuriating in her long, silky fur. Friday purred, rubbing her head against Joan's hip.

"Hey, kitty," said Brandon, reaching out his hand to pet Friday.

Joan turned her head to study him. Brandon's pale skin looked even whiter than usual, contrasting strongly with a brand-new set of dark circles under his eyes. He hadn't put his glasses on yet, and his face looked naked and vulnerable without them.

"How'd you sleep?" she asked. "You look awful."

He gave her a rueful grin. "Gosh, thanks, babe." He grabbed the dark-rimmed spectacles from his own nightstand and made a show of putting them on and examining her. "You, as usual, look amazing with your bed head and the pillow creases on your cheek."

She smoothed down her hair instinctively, and his grin widened.

He caught her hand in his. "No, really, I love it. You're beautiful in any state."

Brandon sat up and stretched, startling Friday, who scampered off to investigate her food dish on the window sill. Joan took a moment to admire the ripple of his lean body, the dragon tattoo on his chest undulating as though flying across a bleak sky.

"To be honest, though, I didn't sleep well at all. I had the most fucked-up dreams," he said.

Joan took his hand and began to massage his fingers and wrists, which she knew were perpetually sore from years of bartending. "What kind of dreams?"

He gave her a sweet smile. "Mm, that's nice, babe, thanks. I was being chased all over town by someone I couldn't see, and the whole time I was looking for you and Sadie and I felt like I was getting so close, but never actually finding you. And then, at some point, it changed to where I was looking for Sadie's twins, like they'd been kidnapped, which is so much worse than thinking that you and she were in trouble. I mean, not that I wasn't frantic about you, but you can take care of yourself, and they're just kids, and—" He stopped.

"Of course. That does sound awful." She dropped his hand and gestured for the other one. He absentmindedly reached over to her and she rubbed her thumb along the center of his palm.

"Hey," said Brandon.

"Yeah?"

He took a deep breath.

Joan eyed him nervously. This seemed like it was getting suddenly serious.

"I, uh..." Brandon paused.

"Yeah?" Joan realized that her fingers were moving more quickly along his wrist, as her mind raced, trying to predict what was on his mind.

He pulled his hand away and sat up straighter. Words started tumbling out of his mouth, as he twisted his fingers together. "I've been thinking a lot. About us. And I had a chat with Veronica, and I think she's really good at talking to people, and she said I should talk to you, and I just— I know we've been doing whatever for a long time, and it's comfortable, even when it feels sort of off-kilter, but I just want to say that, Joan, babe, I, um, love you?"

He ducked his head and peeked at her, sidelong, his face sort of scrunched up, as though braced for rejection.

Joan stared at him, leaning back against the wall, as her breath abruptly left her body. He was right; they had been 'doing whatever' for a long time, but they'd never said those three words together. Was that crazy? The telling part was, though, that he was also right about it being comfortable. Could such an arrangement ever be comfortable without true love involved? Even more telling was that she was thirty-six years old and had never said those words to anyone. She'd had little relationships here and there, in between, but had always gone back to Brandon.

Obviously, she loved him too.

She realized that Brandon's posture had relaxed, and a broad grin spread across his face.

"I was narrating again, just there, wasn't I?" she said.

He grabbed her hand again. "You're an amazing narrator, babe."

Joan flipped over on top of him, savoring the feel of his body beneath hers. She lowered her face to his, stopping just short of his lips. "I love you too," she whispered, and closed the gap, kissing him softly but thoroughly.

BRAP. BRAP. BRAP. Her alarm clock blared, jarring her straight out of the kiss.

"Oh, for the love of God, turn that thing off," moaned Brandon.

Joan grabbed the clock and threw it across the room. The sound continued.

"Has that ever worked?" Brandon groused, as Joan jumped up and rushed to turn it off properly.

"No," she admitted. "It's just instinct."

She sighed with a rueful smile. "I guess the moment's over, huh?"

"We should probably be getting up anyway," he said. "We have to go to Idaho today, remember?"

CHAPTER 10

"Is that the last of it?" Veronica asked.

Joan surveyed the green paper bags packed among their luggage in the cargo area of Veronica's SUV. They were headed for one of the strictest states about marijuana — they didn't even allow it for medical purposes. They could do serious jail time for buying or selling pot there, but they wouldn't have any connections to do so anyway.

And they had no idea how long it would take them to find Wendy or how long they'd be in Idaho.

So they'd stocked up, to the full legal amount they could buy — five ounces of smokable weed, five pounds of edibles, and ten liters of infused sodas.

"I hope it's enough," Joan said, slamming down the hatch. "We'll be no good against Wendy if we can't see."

"Honestly," said Ed, "I kinda think it's overkill." He took a hit off the joint he was holding and offered it to Veronica. She hesitated, then accepted it, exploding into a coughing fit as soon as she inhaled. She handed it back and Ed pinched it out and slid it into the pocket of his grey work shirt.

"Damn," said Brandon, eyebrows raised. "You know you have a lot of pot if Ed Lockhart thinks it's overkill."

Joan pulled open the door to the backseat and slid into the middle. They'd played rock-paper-scissors, and she'd lost.

Veronica sat in the front with Finn while Ed and Brandon bracketed Joan.

As the guys got in beside her, Joan leaned to her left, snuggling up against Brandon, a glow filling her heart as she remembered their conversation that morning.

She took a deep breath in. The air in the car was rapidly filling with the skunky scent of cannabis at rest.

Finn took off, following the directives of the robotic GPS voice out of town.

Five minutes later, Joan was asleep, her head leaning against Brandon's shoulder. She dreamed of first grade.

It was the day after the curse, and somewhere in her mind, adult-Joan knew that she hadn't gone to school that day, but had still been in the hospital along with most of her class as doctors frantically worked to uncover the reason for their collective blind- and muteness. Mrs. Olsen had been in a coma in the same facility.

But in the dream, she was at school, her vision fading in and out as Mrs. Olsen stood in front and assigned homework in their reading workbook. Sadie sat in the desk next to her, Ed, Beth, Veronica, and Derek occupying the other seats. Brandon wasn't there, nor was anyone else from their class.

The potted plant from Wendy's back porch sat on Mrs. Olsen's desk beside her pencil cup and a stack of leather books.

Dream Joan wasn't too worried about the intermittent blindness, and her classmates seemed calm as well, going about their business all around her. In her workbook, she read a silly one-page story about a dog whose food dish was missing. She had to pause occasionally as her vision blurred and continuing when it returned. The story ended with the dog cornering its owner and demanding answers. The human finally gave the dog back its dish.

When she finished reading, she looked at the questions on the other page, designed to help the children's reading comprehension.

What is the symbolic significance of the food bowl?

How could the dog have resolved the issue more peacefully?

List all of the items on your teacher's desk.

What kind of bastard human hides a dog's food bowl anyway?

Suddenly, Joan threw down her pencil with a petulant frown. She didn't need to do this. She already knew how to read. She squinted at her teacher, who was seated at the front of the class, absorbed in a large book open on her desk.

Joan looked around the room and saw that Brandon had replaced Sadie in the desk beside her. He was watching Joan, and as he saw her looking at him, he pointed toward Mrs. Olsen. Joan frowned at him and tried to speak, to ask why he was pointing. Her voice wouldn't work so she just shook her head at him. He sighed and disappeared, leaving the desk empty.

Joan's own seat was in the front row, right by the wastepaper basket, so she threw the workbook away and pulled out her coloring book and crayons.

The dreamscape shifted, as dreamscapes do, to that afternoon. Her dad was picking her up from school and they stood beside Mrs. Olsen's desk. Mrs. Olsen was waving the discarded workbook in the air. "This child is no good! I can't teach her anything if she doesn't do her homework. I need students who respect me."

"Well," Joan's dad replied, "my daughter needs a teacher who doesn't fly off the handle and place curses at the slightest provocation."

Dad's never used the word 'provocation' in his life, protested a voice in the back of Joan's mind. *And those questions were far too advanced for first grade.*

In her dream, her father continued, "And frankly, if you don't release her from that curse this minute, I'm going straight to the superintendent."

Mrs. Olsen looked directly at Joan and her lips curved slowly upward in a cruel, knowing smile. "It's getting closer now. One score and ten. You'll never find me, you despicable little homework-shirker."

Joan shrank back, looking away, focusing instead on the books on her teacher's desk, next to the pot plant. They were large, old leather-bound books, the top volume decorated with a tree, done in Celtic knotwork. Where had she seen that tree before?

Joan woke up with a start, the inside of her mouth cottony and her neck aching from the awkward position against Brandon's chest. Her vision was fuzzy, but she squinted to see that the car was rolling to a halt in the parking lot of a Taco Time restaurant.

"Where are we?" she whispered.

She nudged Brandon awake and he sat up slowly, yawning. On her other side, Ed was engrossed in something on his phone.

Veronica twisted around to peer back at them. "Somewhere in eastern Oregon — it's been all desert for ages. It's about lunchtime, so we figured we'd stop, smoke, and eat. Did you have a nice nap?"

Joan shrugged, trying to shake an uneasy feeling that there was something important in the dream that she was missing. It was just a dream, though, right?

She absently accepted a pipe from Veronica, taking two quick hits and passing it to Brandon.

CHAPTER 11

The *Welcome to Idaho* sign loomed in the distance, and Joan fidgeted nervously as Finn started to slow down. They'd been whizzing along at Californian speeds all day, cutting two hours off of the GPS's predicted timeline. But they'd have to be careful not to get pulled over in Idaho with all this weed.

They crossed the border, and a heavy tan sedan peeled out from its hiding spot behind the sign, blue and white lights flashing. A siren chirped.

Ed inhaled sharply. Joan could feel his shoulders tensing beside her, and heard his breathing quicken. She glanced at him and saw panic written across his face. His eyes met hers.

"That was fast," Ed said, shakily.

"It'll be okay," said Joan, trying to remain calm. Her own anxiety levels were rising and her heart raced, belying the words. She grabbed Brandon's hand for comfort. His eyes were wide, and he looked as terrified as she felt.

"Just keep calm," she said. "It'll look worse if we're freaking out."

"I'm sorry, guys," said Finn, voice tense and bewildered as they eased the car over to the side of the deserted highway. "It looks like the speed limit lowers at the border, and I didn't see it until it was too late. I slowed down to Oregon speeds, not Idaho."

"Not your fault," said Veronica.

"I think we'll be okay if we just stay calm. Calm is the way to get through this," said Finn as the officer sauntered over to the car.

The gruff, bearded man was wearing a sheriff's uniform, a blue and yellow star-shaped patch sewn to the sleeve of his khaki shirt. He stooped, squinting in at Finn, and tapped on the window.

"Roll it down," said Joan. "And everyone try to look casual."

She forced her face into what she hoped was a neutral expression, unwidening her eyes and taming her lips into a small smile — not too big, not too panicky.

Finn pushed the *down* button and then immediately hit it again, lowering the window just an inch. Joan breathed a little easier. Finn seemed to be keeping their head. Maybe the cop wouldn't be able to smell the pot through such a small opening.

"Yes?" said Finn, their voice impressively calm and even. "What seems to be the problem?"

"I'm gonna need you to open up just a little bit more, ma'am."

Finn winced at the feminine honorific, but rolled the window down another inch.

The officer sighed and rolled his eyes. "Suit yourself. License and registration, please." He peered through the window, his eyes roving toward the back seat, as Finn pulled a wallet from their back pocket and Veronica dug in the glove compartment for the registration. "Sure are a lot of you in there. What brings you to Idaho?"

"Visiting an old friend in Luzern," said Finn, sliding the documentation through the window.

"Oh, yeah? Good weekend for it." The cop grabbed the registration, but Finn's license fluttered to the ground. He bent over and picked it up. "This would be a lot easier if you would just open your dang window, Miss . . . Vance."

Veronica leaned over. "We don't have to do that. We know our rights. And it's not 'miss,' officer. Check the gender on the ID."

Joan closed her eyes, feeling her neutral expression slipping. She couldn't blame Veronica for being protective of Finn's feelings, but was this really the time to make waves? The sheriff didn't seem to have noticed the smell yet, and having California plates wasn't technically a crime, even in Idaho. All they had to do was get through this and drive away at exactly the speed limit and they'd be in Luzern in half an hour.

"Well, now," the officer's voice had unexpectedly softened. Joan opened one eye to see that his suspicious frown had faded. She opened the other eye.

The sheriff pushed his broad-brimmed hat back on his head as he examined Finn's license. "You got one of them X's there. I gotta tell you, I wish we had that option around here and the attitude of acceptance to go along with it. I got a nephew — well, I guess not really a nephew, if you take my meaning. My sister's kid. Teenager. He — they — are gonna move away as soon as they graduate, probably down your way, to California, I just know it. Dang shame. Folks here can be a bit behind the times, but it just about breaks my heart every time my sister calls me up, tells me her kid got picked on again. There's nothing I can do about it, and I wish there was."

He passed Finn back their documents, and then fished in his breast pocket for a business card and handed it through the window. "You get into any more trouble with the law, you go ahead and give this to the officer in question. You tell them Deputy Bert Wood has your back."

Deputy Wood turned to leave and then returned to the window. "And air out your dang car. You know that stuff's illegal here, right?"

He ambled back to his cruiser and drove off.

CHAPTER 12

The five of them sat in stunned silence, watching Deputy Wood's car disappear into the distance. Suddenly, Joan realized she was clutching both Ed and Brandon's hands. She tried to drop Ed's, but he just gripped hers harder, his fingers digging into the sides of her hand.

Joan glanced sideways at Ed and saw that he was white as a ghost, his body rigid and his eyes clenched shut. "Hey," she said, nudging him gently and trying unsuccessfully to shake his fingers loose. "It's okay, Ed. He's gone."

Finn turned around, a broad grin adorning their face. "We're okay! That was so awesome!"

"I can't believe we're not on our way to jail," Joan agreed. "You handled that perfectly, Finn.

Finn bobbed their head in a slight bow. "I'm glad I could earn my keep somehow, even if I didn't really technically *do* anything."

"What are you talking about?" said Brandon. "If it wasn't for you—"

"Right, but I didn't do anything. He let us go because of something I am, not something I did," Finn pointed out.

Joan shook her head. "Actually, you were great. I honestly think we had a chance anyway. You kept your cool, and that's key."

Ed finally exhaled a shaky breath and relaxed his death grip. Joan flexed her hand and turned her attention back to him. His eyes were open, some of the tension in his face had eased, but he still looked pretty freaked out. She frowned, concerned. "Are you going to be okay?"

He nodded. "I gotta smoke something."

"Is that a good idea?" Veronica twisted around to peer back at him. "I don't know if we can count on two lucky breaks in a row."

"I just had an anxiety attack and managed somehow to suppress it and not freak out on that cop, but I am going to fucking lose it if I don't get something to calm me down." His voice shook as it spiraled upward in octave.

Brandon unclicked his seatbelt and swiveled around, kneeling on the seat and leaning over to rummage around in the back of the car. "How about one of these edibles or the soda? That way there won't be any visible smoke or smell."

"Yeah, I think that'll work," said Ed.

"And let's get these windows down," said Finn. They hit all the buttons on the armrest at once, and the windows hissed downward, a dry breeze floating through the car. "Deputy Wood was right — we need to air this beast out."

Brandon handed Ed a cannabis-infused soda, and he twisted the top and chugged it. Joan watched, wide-eyed, as he emptied the entire half-liter bottle in one draft.

"Shouldn't we be going now?" asked Brandon, resituating himself in his seat. "I feel like we're just waiting around for another cop to hassle us."

"Yeah, you're right." Finn started the car and headed off toward Luzern.

Ed was breathing easier now. "I know there's no way that it actually hit my system that fast, but somehow I feel better now."

"The placebo effect is wonderful, isn't it, sweetie?" said Veronica.

"Do you guys have an actual plan for when we arrive?" asked Finn.

Joan glanced around at her friends' blank faces. "I guess we just sort of figured we'd wing it."

"And you feel good about that?"

"Pretty good, yeah."

"Give us a break, sweetie," said Veronica. "It's been a long couple of days. We can figure out a plan now!"

"Great." Finn raised a pale blue eyebrow at their partner. "I suggest you do so."

"Well," said Brandon. "The first thing we have to do is get to the hotel and scope it out. See if she's there."

"We could ask at the front desk," suggested Joan.

"Naw, they won't give out that info," said Ed. "We could just stand in the middle of the parking lot and shout."

Or," said Finn, "you could look for her car. Do you know what her car looks like?"

"Yes!" Brandon flung his arm out in his enthusiasm, whacking Joan in the side of the head.

"Ow!"

"Sorry." He planted a kiss on her head and she couldn't help but smile back at him, even though she was officially still annoyed.

"Well? What kind of car does she drive?" Joan asked.

"Blue! Not dark or light blue, just regular."

Finn's other eyebrow rose, their green eyes staring into the rearview mirror at him. "And . . . make? Model? Dare I ask for a year, perhaps, as well?"

"I'm not really a car guy." Brandon shrugged.

"Can we at least get a general shape? Is it a sedan?"

"Um..." he responded.

"Like not a truck or an SUV or a van," they clarified. "A sedan."

"Oh, yeah, it's just a regular car." He nodded vigorously.

"Great," said Joan, back to being irritated. "It's a regular blue regular car. That should be a snap to find in a crowded lot."

"How crowded can it be?" asked Ed. "I mean, Luzern, Idaho isn't exactly a hopping destination, is it?"

"Probably not," Joan conceded.

"Oregon plates, too, right? That should make it easier," Veronica pointed out.

"No, Idaho plates," said Brandon.

Joan glared at him. "You didn't think to mention that before?"

He shrugged. "I just remembered."

"Okay, so we look for her car. What happens if we find it? What happens if we don't?" prompted Finn.

"I say we send Brandon in as bait," said Joan. "Just lean him against the regular blue regular car and see what happens."

He shot her the look he usually gave drunk women who tried to grab his ass at work. "Or we could send Finn door-to-door, since Wendy doesn't know them, and see if we can figure out which room she's in." He snapped his fingers. "You could pretend to be selling vacuum cleaners!"

"Oh, I hate that idea," said Finn. "That sounds like way too much interaction with people I don't know."

"Also, why would anyone be selling vacuum cleaners at a hotel?" said Ed.

"Because the hotel is so clean, and you could just say that it's because of your vacuum cleaners," said Brandon.

"Maybe no one has to be bait. Maybe I could sense her energy," suggested Veronica. "I mean, since she's a witch and all, with witchy energy."

"Could you do that before?" asked Joan.

"No," Veronica admitted. "But I wasn't trying. And I didn't know I could block her spell before either. I just kind of did it. It can't hurt to try, right?"

"Let's call that Plan A," said Finn. "Brandon as bait is Plan B, and me interacting with people is Plan C."

Joan smiled sweetly at Brandon. "Sounds good to me."

"And once we find her?" asked Ed. His voice was much steadier than it had been before. "What's the plan then?"

No one spoke for a moment. Joan realized she literally hadn't thought past finding Wendy. She smiled as her mind entered a fantasy in which she walked right into the witch's hotel room, punched her in the mouth, and said, "That's for kidnapping my boyfriend, bitch." Then, as the witch cowered before her, she would demand, "Now remove this curse immediately!"

And Wendy would nod timidly and wave her hand, and the curse would be gone, and life would be normal, and she could go home and return to work and she and Brandon would live happily ever after.

"That's sweet, babe," said Brandon, taking her hand and squeezing it.

"Dammit, was I narrating again?" Joan closed her eyes and sighed. "I have got to stop doing that!"

"Does anyone have a more realistic idea?" asked Ed.

Joan opened her eyes and glared at him. "It's not that unrealistic."

"Yeah, because she definitely seems like the type to just cower before you and not, I don't know, throw a magic spell at your face if you punched her." Ed rolled his eyes.

"I punched her really hard!" Joan twisted in her seat, dropping Brandon's hand and exerting the full force of her glower upon Ed's person. "It could happen!"

"Are you a martial arts expert?" he inquired. "I've taken some karate classes, and I'm pretty confident in my ability to kick some ass, generally, but I feel like I would think twice before punching a powerful witch in the mouth."

"Is she even that powerful, though?" asked Joan. "Mrs. Olsen was, but is Wendy? She didn't even know her mom until a couple years ago, right? Maybe she didn't even learn magic until then."

"That's a big-ass maybe," Ed countered. "You wanna risk all our lives on it?"

"No," Joan said, reluctantly. "Who died and made you king of logic?"

"Your mind did, apparently!" he snapped.

"You're grumpy today," she muttered. It was a good thing Sadie wasn't there. She had a real thing for argumentative men.

"What's our goal?" said Veronica, twisting around to peer into the back seat. "I mean, why are we looking for Wendy? Are we trying to overpower her? Or is this more of a fact-finding mission?"

No one answered for a moment.

"That seems like something we should figure out," said Brandon.

"Well," said Joan after a moment of reflection, "I think we should kidnap her, tie her to a chair, and waterboard her until she tells us how to undo the curse."

"That seems excessive," said Ed. "Maybe we could just ask her without the tying up."

"And the logic is gone," Joan retorted. "What makes you think she would tell us? Last time we saw her, she kidnapped Brandon!" She gestured for emphasis, whacking the edge of her hand into the back of Finn's seat.

"Hey!" they protested. "Let's keep the area around the driver's seat a no-flailing-of-the-arms zone, shall we?"

"Sorry." Joan turned her attention back to Ed. "We need to be tough with this witch. Catch her off-guard."

Veronica peered back at the them again. "What if she's already expecting us? What if she meant for us to find that email?"

"Whoa," said Brandon. "Like, what if she planted it!"

"How would you plant an email?" asked Joan. "It came from the hotel's email address."

"Yeah, but you could plant the laptop and arrange for it to open right up onto the email," said Ed. "The email could be real, but she just really wanted us to find it."

Joan shook her head. "No way. It was password-protected!"

"Then how'd you get in?" Brandon frowned at her.

"It was a really easy password," she admitted.

"Aha!" Veronica thrust a triumphant finger toward Joan's face. Unfortunately, this was also in the general direction of Finn's personal space too.

"What did I just say?" they demanded.

Veronica lowered her finger meekly. "No-arm-flailing zone."

"Right. That means you too, princess."

"She has a point, though," said Ed. "What if the password was just there to lull you into a false sense of security?"

Brandon chortled.

Joan cocked her head around, puzzled. "What's so funny?"

"Security."

The group stared at him, Finn raising their eyes to the rearview mirror, brows furrowed.

He grinned widely. "It's a funny word! Say it!"

Joan said it, slowly. "Security. Sec-uuuuuuuuuuur-ity. Seeeeec-urity. Securiiiiiiityyyyyyyyyyyyyyy."

"Huh," said Veronica. "That does sound funny. Can I try?"

Joan nodded solemnly.

"Security," said Veronica. Then she said it really fast. "Securitysecuritysecurity." She clapped her hands, bouncing a little in her seat.

Finn snapped their fingers. "Princess! Can we focus? I think it's really unlikely that the email was a trap, but we should probably be prepared for that. Also, speaking as the most . . . level-headed one here, I think we should be treating this as a fact-finding mission, with as little actual contact with what's-her-name as possible. No kidnapping and definitely no waterboarding or anything else that's been banned internationally. I recommend we find her room, wait until she leaves, and then search it."

"We did that already with her house," complained Joan. "I want action! I want this bitch to pay! And, dammit, I want this curse off of me!"

Brandon began to slowly applaud, and Joan jumped, startled, at the first sharp clapping sound.

Veronica joined in, clapping more quickly. "Yeah! Let's fucking settle this!"

Finn sighed. "I mean, you guys are gonna do what you're gonna do, but I just really feel like— Oh, fuck!"

Joan lurched forward against her seatbelt as Finn slammed on the brakes. She lifted her head, peering through the curtain of her hair at the line of cars stopped in front of them.

Then her attention caught on her hair; it looked just like honey. She tipped her head to the side, rolling it back and forth to swing the strands of silky hair across her face. It didn't feel like honey. She sniffed. It didn't smell like honey. It still smelled like strawberries.

"Is everyone okay?" Finn asked shakily.

Joan stuck out her tongue to taste the hair, but she couldn't get the angle right, no matter how vigorously she shook her head.

"Yeah, I'm good," said Ed.

"Just startled," said Brandon. "Joan, what the hell are you doing?"

"Hair is so weird," said Joan. She looked around at her friends, who were all staring at her. "Why did we stop? Is there an accident up ahead?"

Finn grabbed their phone, frowning at the GPS app. "I don't think so. It usually tells you about those kinds of things. This must be . . . normal traffic?"

"Google Luzern," Ed suggested. "Maybe it's not the podunk town we pictured. Just because we've never heard of it doesn't mean it isn't bigger than we thought."

Joan frowned. "No, I looked it up on Wikipedia last night. Ten thousand people."

"Why does a town of ten thousand people that isn't close to a freeway even have a major chain hotel?" Ed wondered.

Finn read aloud from their phone. "Luzern Basque Shepherd's Festival. It's this weekend. Holy crap. 'Due to our exciting musical lineup, we're expecting even more than last year's twenty-five thousand attendees.'"

Ed whistled. "Damn. So the town has effectively more than doubled in size, just for this weekend? That is...going to complicate things."

"We might not be able to find her," said Joan.

"Or," Brandon pointed out, "when we find her, it might be easier to deal with her in all the commotion. Cops'll be distracted."

"Okay, but you still don't know how you're going to 'deal with her,'" said Finn, exasperation clear in their voice. "And really there will be more cops around for a festival. They probably bring in private security—"

They paused with a sigh as Brandon, Joan, and Veronica snickered.

"So there may be extra eyes on festival-goers," Finn finished.

"Do you think she's a festival-goer, though?" Ed asked. "It seems unlikely, doesn't it, that she ran away from a botched kidnapping just to go to a Basque festival?"

"She must be there for some other reason," breathed Joan. Her mind raced. "Do you think—"

No, it couldn't be.

"What?" said Brandon, leaning over to study her face. "What are you thinking, babe?"

"Don't call me that," she replied, automatically. "I bet Mrs. Olsen lives in Luzern."

Chapter 13

"Shut the fuck up!" Veronica shrieked, stopping her arm just in time before it entered the no-flail zone. She settled for kicking her legs back and forth excitedly.

Joan ticked points off on her fingers. "She has Idaho plates. Even though she grew up in Oregon and currently lives in Oregon. She said she reconnected with her mom a couple of years ago. What if she moved out here during those years and only recently moved back to Oregon just to find us? She's fleeing here now, for no discernabuble- discerniale- no clear reason. She must know people here because she was able to get a hotel room, even though I bet they've been booked for months—"

Brandon interrupted. "Yeah, but why is she staying in a hotel at all? Why not stay with her mom, if she lives here?"

Joan shrugged. "Maybe she has a studio apartment. How should I know?"

Veronica shook her head. "No, that's weird. Surely she'd crash on her couch or something, even so."

Joan deflated and Brandon slung an arm across her shoulders, drawing her close.

"It was a good theory, babe. Just full of holes."

"It was one hole," Joan muttered. "Not full of holes."

As the car inched forward, they all fell into a hush, deep in thought.

Joan tried furiously to think of why Wendy would stay in a hotel. She just knew Mrs. Olsen was here. She knew it in her gut, like Veronica had known that Wendy's house was empty. Maybe Wendy didn't want her mother to know about her failure. She came into town to be close to her but wasn't going to make her presence known until she'd come up with a way to frame the events of the last couple of days in a positive light.

Of course, the appearance of Joan and company might actually be helping her save face. If they were walking into a trap, or even if they weren't but totally fucked it all up, and Wendy managed to recapture one of them....

Joan resolutely pushed that thought aside.

"Hey," said Ed, abruptly breaking the silence. "Did we book hotel rooms for ourselves?"

"Um," said Joan. "I guess I figured it wouldn't be an issue. Because who comes to a town like Luzern?"

"A crapload of admirers of Basque culture, apparently," said Brandon glumly.

"So what are we going to do?" Veronica demanded. "I do not camp, I will tell you that right now. Not a camper."

"It's true," Finn affirmed. "We went once with my sister. It was a disaster. Honestly, I'm not big on wilderness either, but Veronica spent the entire night screaming every time a bug moved."

Joan's lips twitched. "I guess we can sleep in the car. It won't be comfy, but you'll be relatively safe from bugs."

She frowned, noticing a slight hoarseness to her voice. How long had it been since they'd smoked? She needed to start setting a damn timer.

Joan nudged Brandon and mimed smoking. He nodded and handed her a packed bowl from the storage pocket in his door. She lit up. As it made the rounds of the car, she set an alarm on her phone for three hours hence. That seemed to be the general timeline of staying symptom-free.

She tucked the phone into her pocket and leaned against the seat, tilting her head all the way back to contemplate the grey ceiling. Her attention was caught by a tiny pink fuzzball clinging to the fabric.

Gradually, the piece of fluff blurred, growing in diameter until it was the size of a face. Then her vision sharpened and she realized she was, in fact, staring into the face of Mrs. Olsen, back in her dream of first grade.

"And furthermore," Mrs. Olsen was saying, "you should have left well enough alone. I can tell, you know, that you've been reading my book. Spellbooks are not for little girls."

"I couldn't even read it anyway," Joan retorted. "It's about lumberjacks or something."

Mrs. Olsen smirked. "It is not about lumberjacks, you idiot child. That book is the key to everything. *If* you can read it."

Joan felt a sharp nudge to her side and was abruptly returned to the real world.

"Oh, sorry, babe, did I wake you up?" Brandon gave her a rueful smile. "I guess we're going to be in close quarters for the foreseeable future."

She grabbed his arm. "That book! With the tree! Did you bring it along?"

"Yeah." His face was startled. "It's in my bag."

She unbuckled her seatbelt and wriggled around to kneel on the seat, leaning over the back. "Which one's yours?"

He twisted his head around and pointed. "The green one over against the door. But we can't read it, remember?"

"I just want to see something," she said.

Joan extended her arms as far as she could, but they didn't reach all the way to the green suitcase. She brought her feet up to squat on the seat but was still too short. Finally, she straightened her legs, bringing her ass into the air and leaning her entire torso across the cargo area, her feet planted flat on the seat.

Her fingertips brushed the handle and she stretched just a little bit more.

"Nice down dog," remarked Veronica behind her, as she managed to grab it.

"Thanks." Joan tugged on the handle, but it was wedged in with the other bags and wouldn't budge. "Crap. I can't move it."

She wriggled her arms, trying to work it free, to lift it up. Nothing happened so she put her whole body into it, swinging her hips to and fro.

"Hey! Whoa!" said Ed as her hip smacked into his shoulder. "Tight quarters, remember?"

She gritted her teeth. "Sorry. Maybe a little help here?"

Ed and Brandon clicked out of their seatbelts and joined her, reaching out on either side to grab the sides of the bag.

"This is a fantastic view," said Veronica.

"Take a picture then," snapped Joan.

As the three of them lifted the green bag up and out, she heard the click of a phone taking a photo.

"Seriously? You're actually taking a picture of our asses?" She guided the suitcase onto the top of another bag situated against the back of the seat.

Brandon opened up the front compartment and brought out a large padded yellow mailer.

"You said I could," Veronica protested.

Joan grabbed the mailer, turned around, and slid down into her seat. She set it down on her lap and buckled up again. "Are you familiar with the concept of sarcasm?"

"Nope! What's that?"

Joan rolled her eyes and stuck out her tongue at Veronica, then turned her attention to the package on her lap.

She untucked the flap and reached inside, pulling out the leather-bound book, running her hands over the soft brown leather. She traced the gold tree, its knotwork slightly raised. Then she opened it up to the first page.

The list of names had returned.

"Hey!" said Ed. "That wasn't there before!"

"It's back!" said Brandon. "The names are back!"

Joan turned the page again. "And here's the German spell." And again. "And the French one. About the lumberjack."

"It can't actually be about a lumberjack," said Veronica. "That makes zero sense."

"Well, whatever it's about, it's here now."

"But why?" pondered Brandon. "What changed?"

"And what's the same from the first time you saw it?" said Finn. "Something must have changed and then changed back.

"Right." Joan thought back to the day before, coming back from Wendy's house, when they'd first opened up the book.

They'd been in Sadie's car. Maybe it only worked in a car. But the book clearly dated back to before cars. Maybe they just had to be in transit.

She tried to focus on what else this moment had in common with that one, but instead, her mind kept drifting back to her dreams. Mrs. Olsen's face loomed in her mind's eye, that triumphant smirk filling her head.

"You know what else is a funny word?" Veronica broke the thoughtful silence. "Ocelot."

"What?" Joan stared at her. "What even is that?"

"It's an animal!"

"Are you sure? I feel like you just made that up."

"No, it's a kind of wild cat," said Ed.

"How is it relevant now, though?" asked Brandon.

"I was thinking maybe Wendy had a familiar, and there had to be some kind of wildlife present for the book to work."

"But there's no wildlife present now," pointed out Joan. "Nor was there any when we saw it before. And, in fact, your dog was there when we didn't see it in the lab. So that's just nonsense."

"Oh, yeah." Veronica pouted. "Well, I don't know, then."

"Hey!" Ed bolted up out of his habitual slouch. "Veronica, you weren't with us when we opened the book in Joan's lab, were you?"

"No."

"But you were there when Joan and Brandon opened it after leaving Wendy's house."

"Yeah."

Ed shook a finger at her. "You're the whatchamacallit! The common denomin-in-in-ator."

Joan studied Veronica. "Are you sure you're not a witch?"

"I guess, maybe I could be. I am adopted." Veronica shrugged. "Maybe my biological mother was a witch, and I come from a long line of witches, and the book knows it, but I don't."

Joan nodded. "Could be."

She leaned forward to put her face right next to Veronica's. "What's that cat called again, please?"

"Ocelot."

"Ocelot," Joan repeated.

"Ocelot," said Veronica.

"Ocelot," said Joan.

"Ocelot," said Brandon. His face split into a wide grin. "That *is* fun."

"Ocelot," said Ed.

"You guys have to stop," said Finn.

CHAPTER 14

As they drove into town, heading for Wendy's hotel, Joan and Brandon flipped through the book. A few pages in, they found one in English, although the wording and spelling were pretty outdated. The handwriting was different from the first couple of pages they had looked at. "A Spell of Love for to Cast Upon a Young Woman," read Joan aloud.

"How cliché," said Finn. "What do you do?"

Veronica mimed a mocking blow at them. "You better not be hoping to entrance any young women."

"None but you, princess," they promised.

"There's a list of ingredients," said Joan. "They sound like herbs, I guess. No eye of newt or anything. And then a ritual below. You mix them up, 'pressing them upon a pestle,' whatever that means, and then — Oh, my god, there's a dance. With detailed moves."

"What, like The Hustle or something?" said Ed.

"I have no idea. How do you do The Hustle?" Joan asked, raising an eyebrow at him.

Finn and Veronica grinned at each other, and Veronica began to gyrate in her seat. "You step forward and back, and then you spin." She clapped her hands once and then pointed her right finger up and then down across her body diagonally. Then she began rolling her hands over each other first next to her left hip, then her right. "Oh, what's next?"

"The chicken thing!" directed Finn, giggling.

"Right!" Veronica crooked her elbows and put her hands on her hips, flapping her arms like wings.

"Watch it!" laughed Finn, dodging Veronica's left elbow.

"Is that it?" said Veronica. "I feel like there's one more thing."

"I don't know, some kind of flourish at the end," said Finn.

Joan snapped her gaping jaw shut and glanced down at the dance instructions on the page. "Um. No." She shook her head emphatically. "It's not like The Hustle."

"Oh, well." Veronica shrugged. She and Finn continued to giggle and mime disco dances to each other as Joan turned another page. Joan hoped Finn could dance and drive at the same time.

The wording grew more modern as the pages progressed, and more and more of them were written in English. Oddly enough, the newer spells seemed mostly to be about reversing the older ones.

She closed the book on the last page, a reversal of the non-Hustle-based love spell, as Finn turned the SUV into the crowded parking lot of the Luzern Marriot. Joan peered out the window. "Damn, this place is definitely at capacity."

"Well, you never know," said Finn. "Why don't I swing by the front door, and someone can run in and see if there are any vacancies while I try to find a parking spot. If I can't find a spot, I'll assume there aren't any rooms either and pull back around."

"I'll go," Joan volunteered, eager to get out of the car again. She'd always hated long road trips. Her legs had a tendency to cramp up.

The car rolled to a stop alongside the curb at the sliding glass doors to the lobby. Joan unbuckled her seatbelt, and Ed swung open the door. She awkwardly climbed over his legs and lurched onto the sidewalk in front of a scowling young man in a bellhop uniform, who was wheeling a brass luggage cart toward a shuttle bus.

Joan gave him an apologetic smile, and he rolled his eyes and maneuvered his cart around her. She shrugged and headed inside the building.

The lobby was filled with people, mostly families. Many of them were multi-generational, the elderly accompanying younger parents with teens, children, and infants. Joan glanced around and made a beeline past a roaring fire, a snack caddy with tea, coffee, and cookies — she paused for a snickerdoodle — and then to the front desk.

She waited behind a tight-lipped blonde who was texting angrily, tapping each letter with irritated emphasis.

"I can help you over here," a smiling African-American woman in her twenties waved to the blonde, and she marched over. "What can I do for you?"

"I had a reservation," the woman declared, accusation in her voice.

"Okay, and you're checking in?" The clerk's smile never wavered, and Joan wondered if she was some kind of superhero. Customer Service Woman.

The blonde sighed. "No. I *had* a reservation. I need to cancel it."

As though that was obvious, and everyone should have known exactly what she meant.

"Certainly, we can do that. I hope this isn't because of an issue with the hotel?" The clerk tapped her keyboard and then looked back up at her customer.

"No. I have to leave."

"Okay, no problem. What is your name?"

The woman slammed a card down on the desk and Joan flinched.

The clerk maintained her smile and simply picked up the ID. She glanced at it, performed a couple more keyboard maneuvers, and then returned it. "Okay, you're all set. I hope you have a fantastic day."

"Yeah, whatever." The blonde rolled her eyes and stalked off.

"Next," called out the clerk, and Joan hurried forward, her fingers crossed. Was it too much to hope that she could snag Bitchy McBitcherson's room? There was probably a waiting list, and canceled rooms went to those people, right?

Joan beamed at the clerk, glancing at her green plastic name tag. "Hi, Alicia. I do not have a reservation, but I sure would love a room. Any chance such a thing might be available?"

Somehow, Alicia's smile managed to widen even further. "As it happens, we've just had a cancelation."

Yes! Jackpot! Suck on that, anyone who had tried to book online and been turned away!

"I'll take it," she said, struggling to remain calm in the face of extreme triumph.

"Perfect. We'll just need an ID and a credit card. Will this be just for tonight?"

"Um... How long is the room available?"

"The original occupant was planning to stay for four days. And past that, the festival is over, so there would probably be no problem extending your stay."

"Cool. I will go ahead and book for the four days, then." Joan dug in her purse for her wallet, pulling out her driver's license and credit card. She did some mental math — she could probably afford four nights. Even if she couldn't, they wouldn't charge the card until the end of her stay, and she could always split it with someone else.

"Just you?"

"Yes," Joan lied.

"All right, Ms. Sinclair, you are in room 706. Elevators are over there, and here is your key. Go ahead and park your car anywhere in the lot, and have a fantastic stay. Enjoy the festival!" Alicia handed Joan her ID and credit card and a paper sleeve with a key card in it. She looked past Joan, transferring her smile to the line beyond her. "Next!"

Joan hastily gathered up her things and moved aside for the next person, a large pale man with a bushy red beard. She strode toward the door, reveling in her good fortune. As she reached the exit, she stepped aside for a pair of college-aged kids with a strong gamer nerd vibe.

She trotted past them and back out into the parking lot, scanning for her friends. She caught sight of Brandon and waved.

Just then, her phone started to vibrate and beep like a crazed robot and she pulled it out. It was the alarm she had set earlier. Crap. Three hours already? She turned off the alarm and set a new one for another three hours. By the time she'd finished, Brandon had almost reached her. "Hey," she called out. "My phone alarm just went off. Time for 'meds.'"

"No worries," Brandon replied. "The others are smoking in the car, and I brought a cookie for you and me to share."

"Mmm. I love you." She wrapped her arms around his waist and leaned against him.

His face lit up as he gazed into her eyes, his left hand resting on her hip. "I love you too," he murmured. The words hung between them like magic.

Brandon pulled out of the embrace to open the cardboard carton with the cookie. He broke off a piece and fed it to her before taking a bite himself.

It was chocolate chip, and it had an unpleasantly herby aftertaste that made her wonder how Sadie had ever tricked Beth into eating a whole one. Maybe Sadie's had been better made.

Then she remembered how hard Beth had been hit, and she decided she'd better not eat all of it at once.

"Let's save the rest," she suggested, grabbing the cookie and putting it back in its slim box. She stowed it in a side pouch of her purse for later.

"I got us a room," Joan told Brandon, grabbing his hand.

"What? You're amazing! I love you!" Brandon swung her around to face him, leaning down and planting a warm, firm kiss on Joan's lips. "I knew we could count on you."

"I love you too." She beamed. "Honestly, though, it was just dumb luck. The lady in front of me canceled, and I got hers."

"Well, I'm sure you did it with panache."

She smirked. "I sure did. But I told her it was just me because these places always have occupancy rules. So we only have one key for all of us. And I have no idea how many beds."

Brandon shrugged. "We'll just send you back to the desk a couple of times, claiming to have lost your key. They'll give you a new one."

Joan tipped her head up, popped up onto her toes, and kissed him again. He hadn't shaved in a couple of days, and his chin was rough and stubbly. "Mm. You're a genius." She looked around. "Where'd you end up parking?"

"Over there," he gestured vaguely behind him. "Let's sneak off and get some alone time, though. Maybe pick up where we left off this morning? Might be our only chance if we're sharing a room with three other people tonight."

"Oooh, yes please," Joan said.

"Come on." Brandon grabbed her hand and tugged her toward the hotel.

"No, we can't go through the lobby. Alicia will see us." Joan looked around and spied a side door. "This way."

"Who is Alicia?" Brandon asked as he followed her.

"The front desk lady. What if she sees us together and realizes I'm not alone?"

"I mean, I'm sure she's busy, right? Even if she saw you, she wouldn't remember you."

"Alicia is some kind of superhero," Joan said. "You should have seen her dealing with the lady whose room we took. Her smile was unreal."

Joan tugged at the door handle, but it was locked.

"Use your key," said Brandon, pointing to the black plastic slot beside the door.

Joan pulled the keycard out of her pocket and unsleeved it. She pushed it into the slot and waited. Nothing happened, so she removed it. A light flashed red.

She inserted it again and pulled it out quickly. The light flashed red again.

"Son of a bitch," she muttered. "Why don't these damn things ever work properly?"

"Let me try." Brandon held out his hand for the card.

"Oh, 'cause you're some kind of keycard wizard? I can do it." She inserted the card one more time, pulling it out with a flourish. This time the light flashed green. "Ha!"

Joan pulled open the door, holding it for Brandon. As he walked through, she heard someone else approach and she glanced back.

Her eyes widened and her heart began to race at the sight of a raven-haired beauty rummaging in her handbag as she walked toward them.

It was Wendy.

CHAPTER 15

"Dammit!" Joan shoved Brandon forward, rushing through the door and slamming it shut behind her.

"What the hell?" he protested.

"Shut up! Wendy's right behind us!" Joan glanced back through the smoked glass. Wendy was frowning at the door, her keycard in hand, but not moving to open it. She must not have seen who they were and was still trying to figure out why they'd been so rude. Good, they had a little time.

She looked around. They were in a burgundy-carpeted hallway. There had to be a stairwell around here somewhere. There!

Joan grabbed Brandon's hand and pulled him inside. The door was propped open. "Should we go up the stairs or wait here?" she whispered.

"If we go up, and she goes past, we'll miss her," he replied.

"But if we stay here and she goes up, she'll find us," she pointed out.

Joan heard the sound of the door opening. "Shhhhhhhhhhhh."

She tiptoed to the corner, slipping behind the door. Brandon followed her, pressing tightly up against her back in the cramped space. They cautiously poked their heads around the beige door.

Then they hastily ducked back as Wendy walked briskly past them and began jogging up the steps.

Joan looked at Brandon and he looked back, his brown eyes questioning. She could hear the witch's hard-soled footsteps echoing hollowly in the stairwell. She put a finger to her lips and began moving toward the stairs as silently as she could.

He followed. They walked slowly upward, loathe to make any sounds, listening to Wendy's steps. Suddenly, the sounds stopped. She must have exited the stairwell.

Joan looked at Brandon again, her heart pounding. Alarm was written across his face, mirroring her own. They'd lost her. Without a word, the pair began to dash up the stairs as fast as they could, stumbling over the risers, skidding around the corners at the end of each flight.

At each floor, Joan peeked her head into the hallway, wildly turning this way and that, desperately hoping to see the wayward witch.

Finally, on the fifth story, she caught a glimpse of a red blouse and a cascade of sable hair at the very end of the hall, just as Wendy turned a corner.

"There!" she shrieked and then clapped a terrified hand over her mouth.

"Let's go!" Brandon took off down the hall, and Joan followed. They reached the end of the hall, rounding the corner after her, and saw a closing door halfway down the next segment of hallway. "That has to be her room!"

They raced toward it, skidding to a halt as another door opened in front of them. Joan struggled to adopt a casual pace and nonchalant facial expression. The man who emerged eyed them nervously.

Joan gave him a reassuring smile, and he relaxed slightly and headed down the hall away from them. She was really getting good at that smile.

They paused at Wendy's door. Room 503.

"Gotcha," Joan whispered.

Brandon held up a hand, palm out. Joan gently pressed her hand against his in the quietest high five ever. He jerked his head back in the direction they'd come, and she followed him back to the stairwell.

"So much for alone time," he remarked once they were safely inside. "We'll definitely have to go tell the others."

Joan sighed. "Fine. Let's go."

She led the way down the stairs and out into the parking lot. As they emerged back out into the sunshine, she caught sight of Veronica and Ed wandering among the cars, looking lost, and, well, incredibly stoned. She looked around for Finn and saw them striding toward the others, looking stern and exasperated.

She giggled and nudged Brandon. "Look at those idiots."

He didn't reply, and she glanced back at him. He was standing very close behind her, his eyes closed.

"What are you doing?"

"Shhhh." He held up a finger.

She waited. "Yeah, but what are you doing?" she asked again after a moment.

He opened his eyes. "Your hair smells like strawberries!"

She spun around to face him. "I know! It's amazing. Veronica's smells like coconut."

"Ohmigod. What does mine smell like? Quick!" He urgently lowered his head to her nose, and she breathed in deeply.

"I'm getting notes of vanilla," she said. "And something . . . deep and smokey."

"Really? I want to smell it. I'm going to have to grow it out. That's the only way I'll get to be able to smell my hair." Brandon lifted his head, his eyes and mouth drooping, and Joan felt very sad for him.

"You don't have to do that. You can just always ask me, and I'll tell you just what it smells like," she told him earnestly.

"You'd do that for me? Always?"

"Of course." She held up a hand, her smallest finger crooked.

Brandon linked his pinky with hers solemnly. "You can't break a pinky promise. A pinky promise is forever."

She nodded. "Everybody knows that."

Hearing footsteps behind her, Joan turned. Finn had hold of Veronica and Ed's hands and was tugging them along.

"Were you able to get us rooms?" they asked.

Joan held up her keycard. "Well, a room. Only because there was a cancellation."

Veronica pulled her hand out of Finn's and jumped up and down, clapping. "We're gonna have a slumber party! Oh, this sounds like so much fun!"

"That's great news," said Ed. "We've been looking for a regular blue car, and we found so many."

Joan shook her head. "No, no, no, you don't have to do that. We found her room!"

"What do you mean?" said Veronica.

"She almost caught us!" said Brandon. "But then we turned the tables, and we followed her up the stairs and around the corner and around another corner and we saw her go into a room, and we totally found her!"

"That's great!" said Ed. "So what's her room number?"

"305," said Joan.

"503," said Brandon at exactly the same time.

There was a moment of silence as Joan looked at Brandon and Brandon looked back, and the others looked from Joan to Brandon and back again.

"So, you don't know her room number," said Finn finally.

"I mean, it's probably one of those two," Joan said.

"It definitely had a three in it," said Brandon.

"And it must have had a five as well," agreed Joan.

"Do you at least know what our room number is?" asked Ed.

"Yes!" Joan pulled out the paper sleeve that the keycard had come with. She looked at it and held it up to Ed's face. "It's right here." She looked at it again and then swung her outstretched arm around to show Veronica and Finn. "706. So there!"

"Okay, well, I vote we head up there, put away our bags, and make a plan," suggested Finn.

"Yes," said Joan. "Very sensible. Let's grab the bags. Where are the bags?"

Finn led the way back to the SUV and supervised the division of labor, ensuring that each person was laden with the same amount of luggage, and then leading them back again to the hotel's side door.

Veronica skipped ahead, attempting to open it with a crooked elbow.

"It's locked," Joan called. "Gimme a second; I've got the thingy."

Joan hurried forward, staggering a little under the weight of her backpack, and struggling to keep the rolling bag she was dragging behind her from capsizing. She set down the tote full of THC-infused sodas and dug into her pocket to pull out her keycard again.

She repeated the usual rigmarole of inserting and removing several times. Finally, the green light flashed, and Joan pushed open the door with a triumphant grin. She held the door open for the others and then took up the rear. The group paraded down the hall, stopping at an elevator.

They waited for a minute or two. Finally, Joan glanced at the button and realized it wasn't lit up. "Did you hit the thingy?" she asked.

"What?" said Veronica.

"The button. You have to hit the up arrow." Joan reached over, tapping the arrow. The door opened immediately. "It was here the whole time."

Finn herded the group into the elevator efficiently. As they rode up, Brandon kept leaning over and sniffing Joan's hair. Veronica noticed and looked thoughtful. She nudged Ed aside and inched closer to Finn, inhaling deeply.

"What does it smell like?" asked Joan.

"Charcoal," Veronica replied.

"Interesting," said Joan. "In a good way?"

"Very much so."

The doors opened, and they picked up their bags once more and began their trek down the hallway. They didn't have far to go — the room was only two doors down.

Joan opened the door with the keycard — miraculously, it worked the first time — and led the way inside. In her head, as she navigated Veronica's wheely bag across the lintel, she chanted, *Please be a suite. Please be a suite. Please be a suite.*

It wasn't a suite. Joan grimaced as she glanced around the room, which contained one queen-sized bed, a dresser, a desk, and a wooden swivel chair. This was going to be cozy.

"I brought a sleeping bag," said Ed, setting down his backpack and unzipping it. "You guys can fight over the bed."

Joan looked at Veronica. Veronica narrowed her eyes at her. She looked at Finn, who was nervously eying Veronica. She looked at Brandon, who shrugged at her.

"You guys can have the bed," Joan decided. She reached over and opened the closet next to the door. "There are always extra blankets. We'll just make a little nest."

"Out in the car," said Brandon quickly. "We'll make a nest out in the car."

Joan perked up. Maybe they'd be able to get some alone time after all.

"Perfect," said Veronica, bouncing onto the bed.

Finn patted down their pockets. "Oh, crap. I think I left my glasses out in the car." They looked around at the others nervously. "Are you guys going to be okay here if I run out and grab them?"

"We'll be fine, sweetie," said Veronica.

"Okay." Finn opened the door and paused. "Stay here. Don't go anywhere until I get back."

"Of course not!" Veronica reassured, making a shooing motion with her hands. "You worry too much. Go!"

With one more glance back, Finn departed.

Veronica turned to Joan. "Have you guys remembered Wendy's room number yet?

Joan looked at Brandon. He shrugged helplessly. "I guess not."

Ed looked up from his vantage point on the ground, where he was busily arranging his sleeping bag. "We have some options. Finn could knock on the doors. Or we could pick one of the two room numbers we have, ask at the front desk to call Wendy Sharp in that room, and if they say that's not her room, then we assume it's the other one. Or we could watch both rooms and see if she comes out. Or we could go have a drink at the bar and see if she shows up."

"Oh, I like that one," said Joan, perking up. "It's been a long day. Also, I'm starving."

"Yes, I second that," said Brandon. "Do we think this place has more of a mozzarella-sticks-and-jalapeno-poppers kind of bar or is it more of a flatbreads-with-arugula kind of place?"

"Wait a second!" Veronica objected. "Finn said to stay here."

"I'm sure they meant to stay in the hotel," said Joan.

"I'm thinking flatbreads with arugula," said Ed. "And I get a definite badass spinach-artichoke dip vibe."

"Oh, that sounds amazing. With those red and blue tortilla chips?" said Joan. Her stomach rumbled. "Let's go. Maybe they've got some kind of sliders. I love sliders. They're delicious and adorable."

"Like you," said Brandon, nudging her playfully.

"Awwww. You are." Joan opened the door and held it open. Ed and Brandon walked out into the hallway. Joan looked at Veronica, who hadn't moved. "Are you coming?"

"But Finn said—"

"Is Finn the boss of you?" Joan asked.

"No."

"So let's go!"

Chapter 16

"Yeah, but listen," said Veronica half an hour later, setting down a pulled pork slider. "Listen here. Just listen."

"Dude?" said Ed. "We've been listening. You're not saying anything."

"I'm gonna say something!" she insisted. "Just listen to me." After a moment, she shook her head. "You know what, sweetie? I just don't even know how to say it."

Joan giggled. She scooped up some more spinach dip. It was, in fact, a badass dip, even if it had come with pita triangles instead of colorful chips. "Well, I think you made some good points. Especially about whatsisname and the thingamabobber."

She suddenly remembered that they were supposed to be looking out for Wendy, and she glanced around the crowded bar. She saw a few women with black hair, but upon closer inspection, none of them was their witch.

"Hey, where's Finn?" said Ed. "They've been gone for a long time. What did they go back for again?

Veronica straightened up in her chair. "Goodness, you're right. I think their glasses were just sitting on the dashboard. That's a weird term. What does 'dashboard' really mean?"

"Dashboard," said Brandon. "Is it a board made of dash?"

"Maybe it's a board for dashing," suggested Ed.

"Did you bring your phone down with you?" Joan asked.

Veronica pulled her phone out of her hip bag. "They haven't texted me. Do you think I should call them?"

"Yeah, definitely," said Brandon, frowning.

As the phone rang, Joan felt uneasy. It rang three more times, and then Finn's business-like recorded message came through, asking the caller to leave a name, number, and reason for calling.

Veronica hit *End*, anxiety written across her face.

"You go look for them," Joan suggested. "We'll close out our tab and then follow."

Veronica needed no more urging. She surged out of her chair, hurrying toward the lobby.

Joan spotted the server and waved to her. "Can we get our check, please?" she asked.

The server pulled a tablet out of her apron, swiping through a few screens until she arrived at the relevant page. "Together or separate?"

Ed pulled out his wallet. "I got this one."

The server ran his card, and the trio wove their way between the tables, through the lobby, and out to the parking lot. Joan led the way out to Veronica's blue SUV, but there was no one around it.

"That's weird," she said with a frown. "Where the hell are they?"

Brandon peered in through the passenger window and then into the backseat. "They're not inside either."

Joan looked around uneasily. Even if Finn had gone missing, Veronica should still be out here. She had only been a few minutes ahead. "I'll try calling Veronica."

It went straight to voicemail. Veronica's message was considerably perkier than Finn's. "Well, fuck. What do we do now?"

"Look for clues?" suggested Ed.

"Like what?" Brandon furrowed his brow. "Mysterious footprints? We're in a parking lot."

Joan circled the car, examining the ground. Yes, the car was parked on concrete, but they were on the edge of the lot and there was soft dirt in front of the SUV's blunt nose. "Ohmigod, you guys! They're here! Mysterious fucking footprints! I mean, I'm no cop, but this looks like a scuffle, right?" She waved her arm wildly, beckoning to Ed and Brandon.

Unfortunately, Ed and Brandon had already come up behind her when she'd started shouting, so she whacked both of them in the face. They quickly backed up and eyed her warily.

"Sorry. Sorry. I got excited." Joan moved her arms straight down at her sides. "Come on. See? You're safe."

They cautiously stepped forward and looked at the ground in front of her. The ground was covered in footprints and divots, the grass disrupted by deep gouges.

Brandon whistled. "Yeah, actually it does look like a scuffle."

Ed crouched and began gesturing to various spots on the ground. "There are three sets of feet here. All relatively small, belonging to women. Or, as the case may be, two women and one non-binary person who was assigned female at birth, so, you know, has smallish feet. What kind of shoes were Veronica and Finn wearing?"

Joan racked her brain. "Honestly, that seems like the kind of thing Veronica notices. I have no idea."

Brandon spoke up. "You're ridiculous. Why do you never notice what anyone is wearing? Veronica had on some kind of hippy sandal. Chacos, I think. They were blue. Finn was wearing black Chuck Taylors."

Joan rolled her eyes. Brandon was always harping on her to wear nicer shoes. She should have known he'd pay attention to other peoples' footwear. As long as her feet were dry and comfortable, she couldn't care less. Could care less? Which was correct? 'Couldn't' made more sense, right?

"Joan?" Ed was talking to her.

"Yeah." She looked at him blankly.

"What do you think?"

"About?"

"This trail. We were saying we should follow it." He pointed to a set of footsteps and gouges that sort of looked like someone in fancy heels had dragged someone else off to the left toward the back of the hotel.

"Was Wendy wearing fancy heels?" she asked Brandon.

"You seriously don't remember? She had those gorgeous black boots on," he said, his voice exasperated.

"Gorgeous?" Her eyes narrowed.

He raised his eyebrows and grinned at her. "Jealous? Don't worry, my romantic feelings aren't based on boots."

Joan looked down at her own feet. She was wearing beat-up running shoes that she'd bought at a thrift store. The soles were starting to come apart, and she made a note to dig out some glue when she got home and patch them up. "Well, good. Fine. Let's follow gorgeous boot lady."

The tracks led to the back door of the hotel, which Joan opened with her keycard. Once inside, they followed the muddy tracks to an elevator.

"And here the trail ends," said Ed. "It's the modern equivalent of wading in a creek." He raised an eyebrow at Joan and Brandon. "Still don't remember which room it was for sure?"

Joan shook her head. "We'll have to knock on both doors."

"I think Ed should do it," suggested Brandon. "She's less likely to remember him from the lab."

"Yeah, I think you're right." Ed nodded. "Any tips?"

Joan pushed the up button to summon the elevator, thinking over the few interactions she'd had with Wendy. "I guess it'll depend on whether she does remember you. If not, then you'll need a pretense to get into the room."

Ed nodded thoughtfully. "I have an idea. Let's stop back at our room first. I need to grab a couple things."

The elevator doors opened and they trooped in, taking it up to the seventh floor. As the trio returned to their room, and Ed gathered up some supplies, they brainstormed plans for if Wendy *did* recognize him.

The best they could come up with was booking it out of there before she could kidnap him too.

They decided to start on the third floor — Room 305. Joan and Brandon posted up in an alcove a few doors down, peering around the corner and watching as Ed steeled himself and raised his hand to knock.

"This is kind of fun," whispered Brandon, nudging Joan in the ribs with his elbow.

"Fun? Are you crazy?" She turned her head to stare at him. His face was very close to hers, as he crouched beside her. She found herself distracted by the stubble sprouting across his cheek and chin. It gave him a slightly rakish air. "Take off your glasses."

"What?" He eyed her, his brow furrowed in confusion. "Why?"

"I just want to see."

He took them off. "I thought you liked my glasses."

"They don't go with the stubble, though. Mmmm. You look like a pirate."

"Really?" Brandon arranged his face into a mock-scowl. "Arrrrgh."

"No, you're ruining it. Don't be a silly pirate. Actually, maybe don't be a pirate at all because they were really horrible people who perpetuated some messed up atrocities. Maybe you're a smuggler instead." Joan nodded. "Yeah, like Han Solo."

"Han Solo didn't have stubble, though," Brandon pointed out. "Can I be Aragorn? From *Lord of the Rings*?"

"Definitely. Let's see your best brooding face."

"Oh, I know!" He pulled his glass pipe out of his breast pocket and held it to his lips, staring off over her shoulder in a melancholy air, as though the weight of Middle Earth was resting on his shoulders. The effect was slightly ruined by the tie-dye-esque swirls decorating the pipe.

Joan giggled. She was so happy that she and Brandon had finally gotten their shit together and made their love official — she felt like a bride on the weirdest honeymoon ever.

"Wait, what's going on out there?" said Brandon. "We're supposed to be look-outs!"

Joan returned her attention to the hallway, and the smile dropped from her face. Ed was gone.

Chapter 17

"Ohmigod, ohmigod, ohmigod." Joan stared at the empty hall. "We weren't watching. Damn your sexy stubble! What happened to Ed?"

"Do you think she has him?" said Brandon. "Now she has three of us! We're the only two left. Good thing we're smart."

"Are we? We should have been watching!"

"That's true. Dammit!"

Joan shook her head. "No point in dwelling. What's done is done. What do we do now? It must be Wendy's room or he would have just left. So either she recognized him and has him tied up next to Finn and Veronica, or she didn't and he's in there pretending to examine her room for ghost activity."

"What if we knock and pretend to be his crew? And we found ghosts somewhere else, and he needs to come with us."

Joan smacked him lightly on the side of the head. "She knows who we are! You've slept with her!"

"Oh, yeah." Brandon gave her a rueful grin. "I really wish I wasn't high right now."

"And I wish the bar downstairs had been a mozzarella-sticks type of place. Life isn't fair."

"Okay, I have an idea," said Brandon. "Wait here."

Brandon crept down the hall toward Room 305. He squared his shoulders, lifted his hand, knocked on the door, and sprinted back toward Joan, gesturing frantically for her to duck back into the alcove.

She flattened herself against the wall as he rounded the corner to join her, breathing heavily from exertion.

"Dude, are you out of breath? You ran like three feet." She stared at him. "We need to join a fucking gym."

"Shut up! It's a stressful situation is all. Is she coming out?"

Joan peaked around the corner to see the door open. A brunette head peered through the doorway, turning to and fro. Joan ducked back again as the puzzled face turned in her direction. "It's not Wendy!"

"She has an accomplice?" said Brandon.

"No, I don't think this is the right room. I know that girl, though." Joan tried to remember why the young woman looked so familiar. She snapped her fingers. "I saw her in the lobby this morning."

"So, if it's not Wendy's room, what the hell is Ed doing in there?" said Brandon.

Ed's voice drifted toward them. "Naw, really, guys, I gotta go. Thanks for letting me check your room. I got a lot of other rooms to check. Always nice to meet fans. Thanks again. Bye now. Really. Bye!"

Joan looked around the corner again and saw that the nerdy couple she'd seen earlier was now dragging at Ed's arms, trying to haul him back into their room.

"Come on, Mr. Lockhart, there are definitely ghosts in here. I saw one just this morning!" the olive-skinned young man babbled. "She was standing in the corner, pointing at me. Just pointing. Right in here, I'll show you."

Ed clutched his ghosthunting gear to his chest, looking around desperately for a way out.

"Come on," said Joan. "We have to save him from his adoring public."

She strode down the hall. "There you are, Ed. We have a promising lead upstairs. Let's go before it's too late!"

Ed shot her a grateful look. "You heard her, guys. My, uh, production manager found something for me. Gotta run."

Amid vigorous protests, Ed finally extricated himself from their grasp and hurried down the hall toward Joan and Brandon.

Joan paused at the elevator, but Ed kept going.

"Can't stop. They'll try to grab me again," he muttered, continuing on toward the staircase. "I don't have a lot of fans, but the ones I have are super intense people."

When they reached the fifth floor, they huddled into another identical alcove, sitting down on the armchairs and loveseat within to regroup.

"Okay, so if that wasn't her room, that means this one is," Brandon pointed out. "Are we going with the same plan?"

"You got a better one?" Ed raised an eyebrow.

"No, not really," admitted Brandon.

"Okay. Then we go with the same plan. I play me — YouTube ghosthunter extraordinaire, checking likely rooms for ghostly activity. If she lets me in, I look for any signs of Veronica or Finn, or anything generally that might help us out. If she refuses, then we at least know it's her room for sure, and maybe I can listen for voices or whatever."

"And if she recognizes you, then run like hell," said Joan. "Don't be a hero."

"Right." Ed nodded. "Here goes." He exhaled with a whoosh and stood up. "I'm going now." He stood still for another moment. "Yep. Okay, then." Finally, Ed strode out of the alcove and around the corner.

Joan and Brandon looked at each other, then jumped to their feet, rushing to the corner to watch.

Ed raised his hand, made a fist, hesitated, lowered his hand, and glanced back at Joan and Brandon.

Joan gave him an encouraging thumbs up. "You can do it," she whispered.

He nodded, lifted his hand again, and knocked three times. He stepped back, poised as though to run away.

They waited. And waited. And waited.

A good minute passed as Ed shifted from foot to foot. Joan's heart pounded, and she bit her lip. Maybe they still had the wrong room. Or maybe Wendy wasn't going to answer because she was torturing information out of their friends.

"Try knocking again," advised Brandon in a stage whisper.

Ed put a hand to his ear.

Brandon repeated his suggestion, a little bit louder.

Ed shook his head, confusion on his face.

"Oh, for—" Brandon strode down the hall impatiently. He pounded on the door. "Just try again, I said!"

The door flew open, and Brandon and Ed froze in place.

Joan gasped, her eyes wide, heart racing. She ducked back into the alcove, straining to listen for voices in the hallway.

"Brandon!" Wendy's sultry voice was full of joy. "I knew you'd find me!"

Joan's eyes narrowed, and she stuck her head out to see what was happening.

Wendy was hugging Brandon.

Joan took a step forward and then stopped herself. She needed to keep hidden. Brandon could handle himself this time, and Ed was there too. She should stay out of it, wait until the opportune moment, and then intervene. She ducked back out of sight.

"Um, hi, Wendy," said Brandon's voice. "Yeah, well, I was in town, you know, for this festival dealy, and I figured, why not look up Wendy while I'm here, and you remember my friend Ed?"

"Oh. Sure. Hi." Wendy was clearly not happy that Brandon hadn't come alone.

"We actually came in a group," Ed put in. "Maybe you've seen our other friends?"

"Nope. No, haven't seen anyone," said Wendy.

Joan frowned. That was an awfully quick response, especially since Ed hadn't named or described their friends at all.

"Really?" said Ed. "You haven't seen anyone? In this crowded hotel?"

Wendy laughed low in her throat. "I've just been hanging out in my room. It's been so lonely."

Joan could practically hear Wendy's eyelashes batting. She gritted her teeth but stayed put.

"Well, maybe we could come in and keep you company," suggested Ed.

"No!" shouted Wendy.

Joan heard the sound of a door slamming.

"I mean, that doesn't sound like much fun. How about a drink?" said Wendy. "Downstairs. The bar here is great! They have these fabulous flatbreads with arugula. And the spinach dip is quite nice as well."

There was a pause, and Joan peeked around the corner. Wendy was standing very close to Brandon, gazing at him in adoration. Ed stood behind her, gesticulating to Brandon, indicating the three of them and miming drinking. Then he pointed toward Joan and then to the door.

Right. Ed and Brandon would distract Wendy, and Joan would break into the room.

"Yeah, actually, a drink sounds great," agreed Brandon.

Joan gave Ed a thumb's up to indicate her understanding of the plan.

"Great!" said Ed. "Let's go!"

"Oh." Wendy turned toward Ed. "You know, I'm sure you have better things to do. You don't have to come along."

Joan gave Ed a meaningful look. There was no way in hell she was going to let that witch get Brandon alone again. Last time, he ended up zip-tied to a chair in the middle of a pentagram.

"Nope!" he said cheerfully. "That dip sounds fantastic! Come on!"

Ed started down the hall, away from Joan.

"No, the stairs are this way," said Wendy, reaching for Brandon's hand.

"I know a shortcut," Ed insisted. He grabbed Wendy's hand before she could touch Brandon, nervously glancing toward Joan, and began lugging her down the hall.

Brandon turned and shrugged to Joan before trailing behind Ed and Wendy.

"So, Wendy, tell us about your family," said Ed as they rounded a corner at the end of the hall. "I want to know everything."

Joan waited until the voices faded away completely and then stole up to the door. She thought furiously. How the hell did one break into a hotel room, anyway? She twisted the handle, but it was locked, of course. These doors always locked automatically.

She flattened herself against the door, ear pressed against it, listening for any sounds of prisoners inside. She heard nothing, but that didn't mean they weren't in there. Maybe they were unconscious or gagged or something.

Joan pounded on the door, calling out, "Veronica? Finn? Are you guys in there?"

Then she listened again. No voices, but she thought she heard a faint thud. "I'm here, guys!" she called. "I'm going to get you out of there, I swear!"

The door next to her opened, and a dark-complected woman, wearing a light blue hijab, emerged. She stopped as she caught sight of Joan.

"Hi," said Joan. "Um, I got locked out of my room. And my, uh, kids are in there."

The woman frowned. "Won't they let you in?"

"Well, they're really little, you see. They can't open the door."

"Oh, no, that's awful." The woman eyed the door. "I think you can get a new keycard from the front desk. I'd be happy to stay up here and keep an eye on the door, in case your children manage to get it open."

"Oh, yes, well, that's a great idea," said Joan. "But unfortunately, the room is in my husband's name, so they won't give me a key."

"Oh, dear."

"Yes, it's quite a pickle. I think I can figure it out, though, thanks for stopping. I appreciate your concern. You can run along now." Joan smiled desperately. Every second this well-meaning lady stood there was less time she had to save her friends before Wendy came back.

"If you're sure..." The woman looked doubtful.

"Yeah, I just need to get little Susie in there to understand how doors work. She's very smart for a one-year-old. I think I can teach her from here. Thanks so much!"

"Well, okay."

Joan leaned against the door as she watched the other woman walking down the hall, giving her a little wave as she turned back one more time before disappearing into the stairwell. She quickly turned her attention to the lock, examining it carefully, and trying her keycard several times, just in case it worked. It didn't. She flung herself at the door in frustration, sliding down to the carpet and closing her eyes as she sat in front of the door, trying to remember how people did this in movies.

An excited voice came from down the hall. "There she is!"

Joan's eyes flew open, and she scrambled to her feet. Ed's fans rushed toward her.

"You're Ed Lockhart's production manager, right?" said the brunette. "Did you find any ghosts?"

"Uh, yeah," she said.

"In here?" asked her boyfriend.

"Yeah, but I got locked out," she said.

"No problem," he said, pulling off the black backpack he wore and rummaged in it, taking out a flat rectangular black box.

Joan craned her neck to watch as he opened it up and pulled out a small cylindrical device with a USB cord. "What is that?"

"Microcontroller," he said, squatting awkwardly in front of the door and plugging it into the underside of the lock. "Cover me, Desiree."

The girl moved to stand beside him, hiding him from view of anyone approaching from the stairs. She frowned at Joan. Joan shifted so she would block the view in the other direction.

"I programmed it before we got here, to unlock any room in this hotel," the guy continued.

"What?" Joan eyed him nervously. Was he some kind of supervillain? "Why? How? You know what, I don't want to know."

He shrugged. "I was bored. And you never know when it'll come in handy. There!"

The locked flashed green, and he turned the handle, unplugging his tech as the door swung open.

Joan rushed into the room and ran over to Veronica, who was blindfolded and tied to a chair over by the window.

"Holy crap," said Desiree. "What is happening here?"

Veronica lifted her head. "Who's there?"

"It's me," said Joan, crouching behind her friend and pulling her handy dandy corkscrew out of her purse. "You guys check the closet and the bathroom. There might be another one who needs help."

She unfolded the foil cutter and sawed at the zip tie holding Veronica's wrists together. Wendy had pulled it tighter than before, and she had to be careful not to cut into Veronica's arm. As the blade finally sliced through it, she heard a tenor voice from the bathroom.

"Hey, lady, I found the other one. I think you'd better come and look at this."

"I'm coming," she called. She pulled Veronica's blindfold off and then hurried to the bathroom to find Finn standing in the bathtub, pounding on air like a mime. "Finn? What're you doing?"

Finn's face lit up, and they began pounding harder. Their lips moved, but Joan couldn't hear any words.

Veronica rushed up behind her and threw herself toward Finn. She bounced off of thin air, sliding to the floor, clutching her face.

Joan crouched down beside Veronica, and Finn mirrored her actions in the tub next to her. "Veronica, are you okay?"

Veronica nodded. "I think so. What's going on?"

"I feel like you would know better than me!" said Joan. "We followed you out to the car, but you weren't there, and then we saw your tracks in the ground, and then Ed and Brandon distracted Wendy, and I got this hacker dude to help me break into her room—" She gestured toward the nerds who were crowded in the doorway, gaping.

The hacker dude stepped forward. "You can call me Neo."

Joan raised an eyebrow at him. "Neo? Really? Is that your hacker name?"

"No, my parents are really nerdy too."

"He never had a chance," remarked Desiree.

"Oh. Sorry. Anyway, Neo helped me break in, and I untied you and told them to look for Finn, and now here we are." She turned toward Finn, who was kneeling on the floor of the bathtub, a forlorn look on their face. They lifted a hand toward Veronica but was stopped by an invisible wall between the tub and the rest of the room.

Joan poked an experimental finger toward Finn, snatching it back when she touched the wall. It felt sort of ... spongy.

"Is that a force field?" asked Neo.

"I think it's a spell," she said absently. "Wendy's a witch."

"Cool!" said Desiree. "A real witch?"

"Yeah," said Joan. "Only it's not actually all that cool, because she put a curse on us, or her mom did anyway, but she triggered it early, and we've been tracking her down, and hoping we can find a way to lift it." She turned her attention toward the nerds. "So, you guys came prepared with the tech. I don't suppose either of you know anything about magic?"

"Not real magic," said Neo. "Pretty much any system of magic found in movies or games."

"What about the book?" said Veronica. "Did you bring it with you?"

"Good idea," said Joan. "It's in the room. You stay here, and I'll go grab it. Maybe you could try some of your Reiki mojo."

Joan ran down the hallway, slowing as other people passed her and then picking up speed again, pounding up the two flights to the seventh floor, skidding as she rounded the corner, and then sliding to a stop in front of the room.

She pulled out her key card, inserting it several times before it finally flashed green. "It was faster hacking in," she muttered.

Finally, she pulled open the door and rushed into the room. Where was the book? Brandon had it last. Was it in his bag?

Joan dithered for a moment, her hand poised to unzip Brandon's suitcase. "It's okay," she muttered to herself. "We're in love."

But should she start their official love story with an invasion of privacy? "Fuck it. It's not like I'm snooping. This is important."

She opened it up. The book was right on top. She grabbed it and headed back downstairs.

The door to Wendy's hotel room was propped open with a gold sandal, and Joan pushed her way in. She turned to enter the bathroom and stopped short.

"What the hell are you guys doing?" she asked, staring at the assortment of tools scattered around the bathroom floor.

Veronica, who was seated in a lotus position on the countertop, opened her eyes and unfolded her legs, setting her feet on the toilet lid. She leaned forward, bracing her elbows on her thighs, and rubbed her face wearily. "We're trying everything."

"Any luck?" Joan asked.

In answer, Veronica gestured toward Finn who was still in the tub, seated with their back against one end, legs stretched out like they were taking a relaxing bath, in contrast to their face, which was pinched with anxiety.

"Well, you guys keep doing whatever you're doing," said Joan, eying a deadly-looking throwing star lying on the floor next to an army canteen and a Tupperware full of strawberries. "Veronica, let's go into the other room and see if we can find anything in the spellbook."

"Spellbook?" Desiree looked up. She was seated in a corner, assembling . . . something techy. "Can I take a look?"

"Do you speak German or French?" said Joan.

"Yes. Both. And Spanish, Portuguese, Greek - modern and classical, Latin, and Euskara, of course."

"Oh." Joan felt slightly overwhelmed. "What's Euskara?"

The room went silent, as Neo and Desiree stopped their various projects and turned to stare at her.

"It's the language the Basque speak," said Neo, his face creased in puzzlement. "Why are you here, if you're not interested in Basque culture?"

Joan sighed. "It's kind of a long story."

"I love stories," said Desiree, perking up. Neo nodded in agreement, gazing at Joan expectantly, both of them setting down their tools and getting comfy.

"Fine." She launched into the tale of her first-grade curse and the past couple of days, Veronica occasionally interjecting small (usually irrelevant) details.

"So you're not Ed Lockhart's production manager?" said Neo, when they'd finished.

"No, I'm a meteorologist," said Joan.

"Huh," said Desiree. "I took a meteorology course last year, and we basically learned that the weather cannot be predicted. It was a surprisingly difficult class, despite the overarching lesson of futility."

"Yeah, well." Joan shrugged. "It pays the bills. Come help us find a spell to get Finn free."

Joan led the way into the main room, sitting down on the bed with the book in front of her. Veronica and Desiree crowded around her, reading over her shoulder.

"Let's start at the back, where all the undoing spells seem to be," suggested Veronica.

Joan flipped open the book. Good, the writing was still visible. She turned to the last page —the removal of the love spell. That probably wouldn't help. Working their way back, they found an anti-aging spell, a cantrip to remove tarnish from silver, and a way to close a portal to another world.

"Quite a range," commented Desiree.

Joan kept turning pages, growing more and more discouraged. They were getting into the older spells now, and not all of them were in English, so she handed the book to Desiree, letting her flip through while she looked over her shoulder.

"Here!" said Desiree suddenly. "This one, roughly translated, is called 'Dismantling the Glass Box.' I bet this is it."

"What do we have to do?" Joan peered at the page but couldn't read the language.

"It's actually pretty simple, compared to some of those other spells. We'll need some sage, a piece of amethyst, and a drop of blood from the one who is imprisoned within." She looked up from the book. "Hey, Neo," she called.

Neo leaned back through the bathroom doorway. "Yeah, hon?"

"You got any sage?"

"Yeah. The kind you burn or the kind you eat?"

Desiree glanced back down at the book. "Uh, the kind you eat. We have to sprinkle it next to the tub."

Neo disappeared for a moment and then re-emerged, triumphantly waving a ziplock bag containing several spice canisters.

"Perfect," said Desiree. She turned to Veronica. "You seem like a lady who might have a piece of amethyst on you."

She nodded. "I have a small one. Will that do?"

"Yeah, I think so. And now the tricky part. We need some of Finn's blood. I don't suppose you're one of those weirdos who carries around a vial of your partner's blood in a necklace?"

Veronica shook her head as she pulled a purple pebble out of her hip bag and handed it over. "No, but Wendy must have taken some, right? So she could release them whenever she was ready."

"Good point," said Joan. "Remember, Brandon said she took blood from him with a finger stick to trigger the curse." She glanced around the room, and her gaze fell on the mini-bar. "Sadie was keeping our blood in the fridge the other day, right?"

"You guys have some weird hobbies," said Desiree.

Joan raised an eyebrow. "That's rich, coming from you, Ms. Speaks-A-Zillion-Languages, whose boyfriend is Mr. Has-Everything-Under-The-Sun-In-His-Backpack-And-Can-Break-Into-Hotel-Rooms."

Desiree shrugged. "I didn't say it was a bad thing."

Joan rolled her eyes and headed for the fridge. Sure enough, lying on a tray balanced over two overpriced jars of nuts, was a slim vial of blood.

"Got it!" She pulled it out and held it over her head triumphantly. "I don't know how to get the blood out, though. Neo, do you have something that could extract it?"

"I have something that can extract it," said Veronica, pulling her utility knife out of her pocket.

"Fair enough." Joan handed it over.

"Wait!" said Desiree. "So what we need to do is get a little bit of the blood mixed in with the sage. Then put a little bit on the amethyst. And then there's a chant and a dance."

"What is it with these witches and dancing?" said Joan.

"It's pretty simple. Just kind of a ..." Desiree stepped back, still holding the book, and then to the left, and did a little twirl. "And then back the other way."

"Okay, let's do this," said Joan. "Actually, let's have Veronica do this. It might be that you have to have some kind of innate power, and you were able to block Wendy's magic before, and your presence seems to affect the writing in the book. We only get one chance to get Finn free, since we don't have any more of their blood."

Veronica nodded. "Good point." She grabbed the spices from the ground where Neo had placed them, and dug around in the bag, pulling out the sage.

Neo poked his head around the doorway again. "If you could pour some sage out first, rather than just dripping blood into the jar, I'd appreciate it."

"Here," Joan grabbed the canister from Veronica. "Hold out your hand." She sprinkled sage into Veronica's outstretched palm. "How much do we need?"

Desiree consulted the book again. "Just enough to sprinkle in a line across the edge of the tub."

Joan shook a little bit more onto Veronica's hand. "There. Now give me the amethyst."

Desiree tossed her the pebble, and Joan put it into Veronica's hand, nestling it among the sage.

"Might as well just bloody it all up at once," she said. She grabbed the knife from Veronica's other hand and carefully slit the needle-sized plastic vial down the side, holding it by a small uncut portion at one end, above the sage and stone. As crimson blood dripped down, she moved it around, ensuring that some landed on each component. "Now what?"

"Now let's head into the bathroom," directed Desiree.

The three of them inched into the room, careful not to trip over any of Neo's gadgets. Neo scooted into a corner to make more room, gathering tech in various stages of assembly around him.

Finn sat up to watch.

"Put the amethyst in the center of the tub's edge," said Desiree.

Veronica plucked it from the sage with her free hand and carefully placed it.

"Now do the sage in a line, extending on either side."

Veronica slowly began to sprinkle the herb.

Joan was reminded of the pot shake that had formed the pentagram around Brandon's chair in the bar office. She wrinkled her nose as she realized that it must have already been infused with his blood too.

"Okay, what's next?" asked Veronica.

"You have to chant this, while you do the dance I just showed you. 'Desegin, bota, horma desagertu!'"

"'Desegin, bota, horma desagertu!'" repeated Veronica.

"Well, your accent is atrocious, but that's basically it," said Desiree. "Do you remember the dance?"

"It's a forward step—"

"No, a backward step," interrupted Desiree, demonstrating again, kicking a remote control out of her way.

"Right. Backward step, left, and twirl." Veronica did the steps as she spoke them.

"Very nice," said Desiree. "Are you ready to do them together? You'll have to chant as you do the steps and do it three times."

Veronica nodded tensely and began. Her dancing was impeccable, but she stumbled over the unfamiliar words a couple of times. As Desiree began saying them with her, her voice grew in confidence. She repeated the dance and the phrase.

Joan stared intently at the air between her and Finn, but since the wall was invisible, there was no real way to know if anything was happening. As Veronica began her third repetition, Joan reached out a hand and touched the force field. Was there a little more give than before?

Finn took a cue from her and ran their own hand over the wall.

Finally, Veronica finished her chant and her dance.

Joan watched Finn as they continued to run their hands up and down the invisible partition.

And then suddenly, Finn was falling forward as the wall dissolved. With a cry of delight, Veronica threw herself into the tub with her partner, wrapping her arms around them and then capturing their lips in a long, slow kiss.

As the kiss went on, Desiree and Neo began to applaud, Desiree whistling shrilly.

"Okay, you two, break it up," said Joan. "We should be searching the room, looking for clues, etcetera."

Veronica reluctantly pulled herself off of Finn and climbed out of the tub. As Finn stood, they stretched and asked, "Have you decided what, exactly, you're looking for?"

Joan shrugged and strode back into the main room. "Clues. You know. Anything about the curse or about Mrs. Olsen or about witchcraft in general."

Finn and Veronica followed her, Desiree trailing behind, still engrossed in the spellbook, reading as she walked.

"Hey," said Desiree. "You said that it seemed like this witch was completely obsessed with your friend, right?"

"Yeah. They dated a couple of months ago." Joan opened a dresser drawer, but it was empty. She shut it again and opened up the next one. "Why?"

This drawer had some clothing in it. She picked up a slinky sapphire skirt. It was way out of her league, so she put it back, sifting through the clothing to see if anything was hidden underneath.

"They dated a couple of months ago and broke up, and then he didn't hear from her again until super recently, right? And now she's obsessed?"

Joan turned around to look at Desiree. "Yeah. So?"

She held up the book. "I think she might be under a love spell."

CHAPTER 18

"A love spell?" Joan frowned. "What are you talking about?"

"And," Desiree continued, triumph in her voice, "I think we can reverse it!"

"The last page of the book!" said Veronica. "What do we need to do?"

Joan joined the others in crowding around Desiree, looking at the love spell reversal at the end of the spellbook. This one, at least, was in English. But it looked a lot more complicated than the one they'd just done.

"Where are we going to get a sacred dagger?" Joan wondered aloud.

"Oh, I have one of those," said Desiree, digging in her purse.

"Of course you do," said Joan. Why wouldn't she? What woman doesn't carry a sacred dagger in her purse? "And I suppose you have plenty of coriander and a couple of apples in that Mary Poppins bag of yours, Neo?"

"Yep!" Neo pulled out two apples and looked around for his spice bag. He spotted it on the floor next to the bathroom door, where Veronica had dropped it, and picked it up. He selected a canister full of brown powder.

Just then, Joan's phone alarm went off. Time to medicate. She pulled the phone out of her pocket to turn off the alarm and frowned at the screen. She'd missed a text from Ed about five minutes ago.

Joan clicked on the text. *MAYDAY! I went to the bathroom and when I got back, Wendy and Brandon had split. Might be headed your way. Will try to cut them off before they get there.*

"Hey, guys?" she said. "We might have a problem."

She handed her phone to Veronica.

"Oh, crap." Veronica handed it to Finn, who read it and handed it to Neo. Neo tried to pass it to Desiree, but she ignored him in favor of working through the dance moves outlined in the spell.

This one actually did look a little bit like The Hustle.

Joan left her to it, going into the bathroom to snag some of Wendy's hair from the brush she'd noticed in there before. She heard a familiar voice from the hallway and froze in the act of reaching for the brush. It was Brandon! She strained to hear him.

"Look, I really think we should go back to the bar. I mean, I really don't think it's fair to stick Ed with the bill, you know. I mean, he is my friend."

Wendy murmured something in response, too low for Joan to hear. Then her voice lifted. "What the hell? Why is my door propped open?"

Oh, crap. Panicking, Joan threw the hairbrush out into the room and kicked the bathroom door shut. Her mind raced around in circles. As she stared at the doorknob, it began to get blurry. Her sight was starting to go. She heard Brandon pleading with Wendy to go back down to the bar, to go to his room, to go for a walk, anything but going into her room.

Their arguing voices got louder as they entered the room. Wendy shrieked, her voice just on the other side of the bathroom door. "What is going on here?"

"Now!" Desiree yelled. Were they starting the reversal spell?

Joan pressed her ear up against the door, listening to Veronica's voice chanting, "Your false love fades. Cease this charade. This new romance you no longer adore – leave your love as it was before."

Was her voice starting to grow hoarse? Joan listened intently as she began again. Yes, her voice was definitely fading. She opened the door a crack and took in the tableau in an instant:

Wendy was sputtering, wiping ground coriander from her bewildered face.

Veronica was dancing around, waving the hairbrush in one hand, holding a cut apple in her other, and chanting.

Desiree was chanting with her, walking in a circle around Veronica, holding the book in one hand and her sacred dagger in the other.

Finn was miming to Brandon, trying to convey the events of the past half hour to him.

Neo had backed into a corner of the room, trying to make himself as small as possible as he took in the scene with wide eyes.

Joan looked at Wendy again and saw that the witch was starting to recover her senses. And she looked pissed.

Wendy turned slightly to face Veronica, and her back was now to Joan, her hands moving in an arcane gesture. Suddenly there was golden lightning flying toward Veronica.

Joan didn't think – she simply leapt into action. With a wordless bellow, she flung the bathroom door open and charged Wendy, knocking her down and pinning her to the side of the bed. She twisted Wendy's arms up behind her back. Brandon rushed to help her, but the witch thrashed around, struggling to get free, and they couldn't seem to hold more than one arm at a time.

Her long, raven hair ended up in Joan's mouth. Joan's buzz had obviously completely worn off — she didn't even try to taste it. She spit it out, sputtering in disgust.

"A little help here?" she whispered to Neo, who was still standing a foot away, frozen.

His eyes snapped to Joan's face, and he shook himself free of his daze. Neo darted forward and dragged Wendy all the way onto the bed, jumping onto it with her and sitting squarely on the small of her back.

Desiree, apparently finished with her role in the spell, joined him, pulling a length of orange twine out of her purse and wrapping it around Wendy's wrists.

Brandon finally got a hold of both elbows, holding them still.

Joan sat on the witch's kicking legs, stilling them as well, and turned her attention back to the others.

Finn stood between Wendy and Veronica, eyes blazing with fury, hair looking slightly singed. They must have caught the brunt of the attack.

Veronica was still dancing, but her chants had faded. She was still doggedly mouthing the words.

Joan patted down her pockets, looking for some weed, but she didn't have any. How could she have left the room without medication? Because it had been a whole group of them, and Ed had grabbed a bunch. She hadn't thought she'd need any.

Then she remembered — she still had most of that cookie in her purse!

Joan dumped out the contents of her bag on the bed beside her, grabbing the napkin-wrapped bundle from amidst the flotsam that poured out. She broke off a small piece and popped it into her mouth.

Desiree was just tying off the twine around Wendy's wrists, so Joan gestured to her to take over the legs. The girl began to twist the string around her ankles.

Joan stood up, staggering a little as Wendy began to kick again and managed to land one right on Joan's rump. Brandon hurried to grab hold of the witch's legs.

Veronica's eyes fixed on the cookie in Joan's hand, and she broke off another piece. As Veronica opened her mouth, Joan took aim and the cookie flew straight in.

Without missing a beat, Veronica bit down on it, and her voice became a slight whisper. She continued her chant, her voice growing stronger as she chanted with her mouth full. Joan broke off another piece and handed it to Brandon.

Just as Desiree finished subduing Wendy's legs, Veronica wrapped up the dance with a flourish.

The room was silent for a long moment.

"Did it work?" asked Desiree.

"I don't know how to tell," said Joan.

Brandon reached over with both hands and flipped Wendy onto her back. He grabbed a pillow and put it under her head.

Wendy's eyes darted around the room. Her mouth opened and closed a couple of times, her face filled with shock and alarm. Finally, she found her voice – a shrill terrified voice.

"Who the fuck are you people and what do you want with me?"

CHAPTER 19

"**H**uh?" said Joan. Had they done the wrong spell? Was this spell some kind of memory wiper?

Brandon stepped forward and Wendy's head whipped around, her dark eyes rolling back to see who was next to her head.

"Brandon?" she stammered. "Brandon Barber? What is going on?"

"You remember Brandon, but not the rest of us?" Joan frowned.

Wendy turned her head again, studying Joan carefully. "I've never seen you before." As she adjusted to her new surroundings, her voice was descending once more into its customary sultry drawl. She glanced at Brandon again. "I haven't seen you in months. You didn't seem like a crazy person at the time. Why don't you just let me go? I'll never breathe a word of it to anyone."

"Months?" Brandon repeated. "You've been pursuing me relentlessly for the past couple of weeks. You kidnapped me two days ago."

"Kidnapped? I feel like I would remember that," she retorted.

Desiree held up a hand. She was reading the spellbook again. "Okay, I think I know what's going on here. There's a footnote on the spell she was under, which warns that memory might be affected. I guess I missed that when I read it before."

"That's a pretty important detail!" said Joan.

"Well, there was a lot going on. I had just found out that magic is real. Sue me."

"What spell?" Wendy asked, exasperation filling her voice. "I'm not under any spells! My mother runs regular tests to make sure."

The entire room froze.

"What now?" Wendy wriggled up into a seated position, her hands still bound behind her back.

Joan was impressed, despite herself.

"*Your mother* cursed us when we were kids, basically just for being kids," Veronica said, acid in her tone. "And we're pretty sure *your mother* is the one who put a love spell on you. The spell we just reversed — you're welcome, by the way. *Your mother* must have placed the spell so that you'd get back in touch with Brandon. And then *your mother* somehow convinced you to retrigger our curse early and tied it up in the love spell so that now you don't remember any of it. So forgive us if we're a little suspicious of *your mother*."

Wendy stared at Veronica, stunned. Then her gaze fell on the book Desiree was still studying intently. "Is that my family grimoire? Where did you get that?"

"From your house," said Joan.

"You broke into my house?"

"You kidnapped my boyfriend!"

Wendy nodded. "Okay. Let's suppose I believe you, and I'm not saying that I do. But let's just suppose that I did. You guys are from Marion's last class in Alexandria? The ones who attacked her?"

Joan stood up abruptly. "Attacked her? We were six!"

Wendy eyed Joan for a moment and then turned her head. "You. With the book."

She looked up. "Desiree."

"Okay, Desiree. You're a witch?"

"Uh, no. I'm a linguistics major at the University of Idaho."

"A lot of witches are linguistics majors." Wendy raised an eyebrow at her.

"Oh. Well, no, I'm still not a witch."

Wendy looked around the room. "Okay, so who's the witch?"

"You are," said Joan.

Wendy frowned. "I thought you said you did a spell reversal."

Joan nodded. "That's right. We did two, actually. Well, Veronica did them." She bobbed her head toward Veronica.

"So, you're a witch," said Wendy to Veronica.

"Not that I'm aware of."

Wendy shrugged, another difficult feat when one's arms are tied behind one's back. "Well, you've got some witch in you, or the spells wouldn't have worked. And you wouldn't have been able to even see the spells without a witch present. Desiree, if you could find a spell for me in that book — it's a few pages before the end. 'Finding the Truth.'"

Desiree flipped through the pages. "I see it."

"And Veronica, please perform that spell. Let's get to the bottom of this. Take some blood from me, so you'll know that I'm telling the truth, and then one of you give some too, so I'll know you are."

"I'll do it," said Joan. "What do I have to do?"

"We'll just need a little bit of blood from you, and, let's see," Desiree scanned the page. "Neo, I'll need some more sage. Does anyone have the left wing of a crow?"

Joan glanced toward Neo. If he was carrying around birds' wings in his backpack too, she was never going to be surprised by anything ever again.

"Uh, that I do not have," he admitted, as he retrieved his jar of sage from where they'd left it after releasing Finn.

Wendy nodded toward the dresser. "Bottom drawer."

"Seriously?" Joan walked back to the dresser, glad she had only gotten to drawer two earlier.

"It's a common ingredient," said Wendy, a little defensively.

Joan opened up the drawer, and sure enough, among other macabre items, were two crow's wings in a gallon-sized freezer bag. She pulled out the bag. With a glance around the room to make sure no one was watching, she discreetly made L's with her hands to figure out which one was the left. Then she grabbed a couple of tissues from the box atop the dresser and used them to pull out the wing.

"Okay, I've got it. What else?"

"Set it down over here on the nightstand," directed Desiree. "And then we'll get a little blood from you and a little blood from Wendy."

"There's already a cut on my arm from your last spell," said Wendy twisting a little to show them. "It's closed up, but if you squeeze it a little, you should be able to get enough."

"Sorry about that," said Desiree, glancing guiltily at her dagger.

"That's okay. I'd have done the same."

Joan gingerly held the wing next to Wendy's arm, and Brandon carefully re-opened the cut. A few drops of blood trickled down her arm and Joan scraped the feathers against it. Wendy's face remained impassive, almost bored, as though being tied up and having part of an animal corpse rubbed over an open wound was simply an average Saturday.

Neo had his first aid kit ready and wiped the cut with an alcohol pad and covered it with a bandage.

"Thank you." Wendy smiled at the gamer and winked.

He blushed.

"Okay, I don't have to get cut with that same knife, do I?" asked Joan. "That doesn't seem very sanitary."

"No," said Desiree. "This one only requires the blood, not the sacred dagger."

"There are sterile finger sticks in the third drawer," said Wendy.

Joan retrieved one, opened it up, and pricked her finger, squeezing it to drip onto the wing, and then allowed Neo to administer to her tiny wound as well.

By this time, Veronica was studying the book to familiarize herself with the dance and chant and Desiree was just finishing up drawing a mystical symbol on the table around the crow's wing with the sage.

Veronica took a deep breath and got started. This dance involved a lot of arm movements and jazz squares. The chant was in English again, although Joan winced at the double negative. "Tell it like it is. Don't you tell no fibs. Secrets are no fun. Secrets hurt someone."

Joan wondered if the spell was derived from the playground chant or vice versa.

Veronica repeated the chant and dance five times, ending with jazz hands.

Finn giggled at that, and Joan could see that Veronica was struggling to keep a straight face.

"I'll thank you not to mock my heritage," said Wendy, coldly. "These movements have a long and sacred history."

Veronica and Finn sobered.

"Sorry," said Finn. "I didn't mean to offend you."

"No, I'm just fucking with you," said Wendy. "That spell was written by my Aunt Judy, who has a weird sense of humor. I've only met her a couple of times, but I'm not a fan."

"What happens now?" asked Joan.

"What happens now is that most rare of events. An honest conversation." Wendy smiled wryly, and Joan found her own lips twitching in response. Maybe Wendy wasn't such a villain after all.

"Okay, I'll start," said Joan. She launched once again into the story of the curse and the key, ending with a summary of Wendy's own actions of the past couple of days and how they had followed her to Idaho and ended up there in her hotel room.

When Joan finished, Wendy sat in silence for a moment, a cocktail of anger and sadness splashed across her face. She closed her eyes briefly and when she opened them again, her face was composed once more. She inhaled sharply. "Well. I guess my dad was right to keep me from Marian all these years."

"Why do you call your mom 'Marian?'" asked Desiree.

Wendy shrugged. "It's her name. I never knew her as my mom."

Finn sat down beside Wendy and began unwinding the twine around her ankles. "Why don't you tell us your story now?"

Veronica followed her partner's example, reaching down to cut Wendy's wrists free.

Joan stood to make room for them, moving to the chair beside the desk. Brandon sat at her feet, and her hand drifted to his head, absently playing with his soft sable-brown hair. They settled in for the story.

"My parents were brought together by a shared interest: magic. Dad was a mage and Marian is a witch."

Joan's hand stilled as her mind raced. Brandon twisted around and grinned up at her. They'd been arguing for years about multiple forms of magic, and he'd been right. She stuck out her tongue at him and then turned back to Wendy.

"What's the difference?" she asked.

"Magery's learned, witchcraft is inherited," Wendy replied. "Witchcraft uses innate talent, magery uses temporal energy. Witchcraft is traditionally female, magery can be learned by anyone." She waved her newly freed arms. "We're getting off-track, though. All you really have to know is that witches and mages hate each other. Witches think mages are powerless wannabes. Mages think witches are stuck-up and snooty." She paused. "The mages aren't totally wrong, overall."

Joan sank her fingers into Brandon's hair, massaging his scalp, as Wendy continued.

"My parents were young and idealistic, and they wanted to change all of that. They started emailing and then meeting up to study each other's traditions, befriend the enemy, heal the rift, you know the drill. It was all very noble. Marian even transferred to my dad's college so they could meet more frequently."

"And they fell in love?" said Desiree, leaning forward, a small smile playing at her lips, her eyes shining.

"No," said Wendy.

"Oh." Desiree's face fell.

"But they did get really drunk one night while studying a grimoire." Wendy gestured toward the book that Desiree still clutched. "That grimoire, in fact — my family's most prized possession."

Desiree guiltily sidled forward to set the spellbook down on the bed next to Wendy. Then she sat down on the floor next to Neo.

"Thank you," said Wendy. "As you've probably guessed, I was the result of that night. Of course, once they found out that Marian was pregnant, everything changed. They tried to force themselves into becoming a couple." She bit her lip. "Sometimes I wonder what might have been if they hadn't done that, if they had just accepted that they were just friends and co-parents. Maybe Marian wouldn't have gotten so bitter. Maybe my dad would have been happier. I definitely would have been. And who knows? They might even have actually made some peace between witches and mages. Which was the whole point to begin with."

"And we might not have gotten cursed," muttered Joan.

Wendy aimed a sharp glance at her. "Yes. I'm getting to that."

Joan nodded. "Sorry."

"They split up a couple of months after I was born. For a while, they tried the usual joint custody stuff – Dad would take me a few days and then Marian. After a couple of years of this, Marian ran off with me and brought me here to Luzern, which is where she grew up. Dad came after her, sued, and got full custody. He took me back to Salem, and Marian moved to Alexandria. I guess she figured it was close enough that she might be able to see me sometimes, but far enough not to antagonize Dad. She was wrong. Dad was furious with her, got a restraining order, refused to take her calls, deleted her emails. She kept trying, for years. Until suddenly, when I was six, she stopped."

"Because she was in a coma," said Brandon.

Wendy tapped her nose, pointing to Brandon with her other hand. "But my dad and I didn't know that. If I'd been older, I probably would have tried to find out. Dad had no interest in doing so. He assumed she'd finally gotten the hint. I assumed she'd stopped loving me."

Joan found tears prickling her eyes.

Finn took one of Wendy's hands, and Veronica put an arm around her shoulders. Wendy gave them each a tight smile. "Thank you. Years went by. I did have a reasonably happy, albeit lonely, childhood. My dad loved me. He tried to turn me into a mage, but it wasn't really my thing. I wasn't drawn to any branch of time. I knew Marian was a witch — my dad had told me that much — and I wanted more than anything to learn that side of magic. But Dad refused. I turned to Wicca instead, but that's not really witchcraft, just a watered-down cousin."

She paused, turned inward for a moment. Then she took a deep breath and continued. "And then, about ten years ago, Dad died. Turned out that without him around to stand up for me, his family didn't really want me around. I was tainted by witchcraft. Not that I knew anything about my witch side. I felt utterly alone, and I decided to find Marian. I looked everywhere. I even hired a PI, but you know as well as me that she hid her tracks well. Finally, about three years ago, she found me."

Wendy paused again. "I can't describe to you how it felt. I picked up my phone one day and I had a voicemail from an unknown number. I rolled my eyes — I thought it was just another damn robocall. And it was my mom! I had a parent again! And she was so nice. My dad had spent years telling me all about what a shitty person she was, and I was prepared for the worst, but she was— She was nice. And then she started teaching me witchcraft, and I was good at it, and I had never been good at magic before, and that felt amazing!"

She glanced around the room, eyes landing on Joan. "The story she told me about your curse was very different from yours. She said that you guys had turned against her because she was a witch, attacking her en masse, and she was forced to act. I also thought you were older than six. Teenagers, maybe — I can't remember if she lied and said you were or if that's just what I assumed. And then she told me that you'd been trying to find her again and that she was scared. I agreed to move back to Oregon to find you and retrigger the curse."

"Why couldn't she do it herself?" asked Joan. "Why send you?"

Wendy rubbed her temples. "It's all so cloudy. I think it had something to do with the wording. Like she couldn't do anything about it until the thirty-year mark. She didn't want to wait, because she was afraid you'd find her first. I don't even know if that's true. Curses are different than traditional spells, and I haven't been studying witchcraft for all that long."

"So you entrapped me?" said Brandon, his voice tight.

Wendy shook her head emphatically. "No, I didn't! I didn't even know you were part of Marian's class. I had just moved back when we met. I was still settling in, getting a house, starting a new job. I hadn't even started looking for you guys. And she told me to start with Derek Pandora, the most dangerous of you. I guess he was the most persistent in trying to hunt Marian down."

This surprised a laugh out of Joan. All eyes turned to her. "Derek? Dangerous? The man is all egghead."

Wendy shrugged. "Marian told me that Dr. Pandora was dangerous, so that's where I started. When I realized that he wasn't even in the country, I had to start over — going through school records, looking people up one at a time. Honestly, it was super boring and surprisingly difficult to find people, even online. I guess I wasn't giving it the attention Marian thought it deserved. I did some small spells to strengthen the curse, but in order to really retrigger it, I would have to find one of you in person. I guess I wasn't moving quickly enough. I came back here for a visit about a month ago. That must have been when she set the love spell on me. And shortly afterward was when I started hounding Brandon, apparently. I don't remember that at all."

"So, what do you remember about the past couple weeks, sweetie?" asked Veronica.

Wendy turned her head to fix Veronica in a slight frown. "I would really appreciate if you would refrain from using saccharine pet names such as 'sweetie' and 'honey' with me, Veronica."

Joan grinned. Wendy was definitely someone she could get along with.

"I remember coming back to Salem," Wendy continued. "And I remember deciding to put Marian's mission on the back burner. I remember feeling freaked out by her intensity when she was trying to get me to speed things up. I was considering giving it up altogether. I remember going to work, hanging out with my friends, living my life. Nothing else."

An awkward silence followed this, broken a moment later by Finn. "My mom's a piece of shit too. She kicked me out when I was sixteen. She never put a love spell on me or erased my memory, though, so you win."

Wendy smiled at them. "Thanks. I wish I didn't." She took a deep breath. "Anyway, I think I can reverse the retriggering of your curse. I don't remember what I did, but I bet I can figure it out from your description, and then usually you can just sort of recreate it and then switch up the words. But then we'll have to convince Marian to remove the curse itself. Otherwise, it'll still come back in a few months. And probably be worse, because it kind of sounds like at that point she'll be able to tinker with it."

"Great," said Joan. "That's exactly what we've been trying to do for the past twenty-nine years."

"Yeah, but now you know where she is. And you have me on your side," Wendy pointed out. "The biggest thing we need is cannabis. Marian was using it for her headaches when she cursed you, and she told me to use it when I was doing the strengthening spell."

"Your first-grade teacher was stoned?" said Neo. "That's crazy."

Joan raised an eyebrow. "You think it's crazy that she was smoking pot, but not that she cursed us?"

Neo shrugged. "I don't know. I guess my daily life involves a lot more stories about magic than about drugs."

"It's just a plant," said Brandon. "It's legal where we live."

"It wasn't when you were in first grade," Desiree pointed out.

Wendy cleared her throat. "Come on, guys, let's focus. Does anyone have any pot?"

"All I have is the rest of that cookie," said Joan. "Will that do?"

Wendy hesitated. "I'm not sure. To be safe, I think we'd better work with the herb itself. None of you has any on you?"

"Ed usually does," said Veronica. She looked around the room. "Where is Ed?"

Joan realized with a start that she hadn't heard from Ed since his text, right before Wendy and Brandon had arrived on the scene. That was almost an hour ago. Shouldn't he have been heading this way right on their heels?

"Has anyone heard from Ed?" asked Finn.

Joan, Brandon, and Veronica all pulled out their phones, but there were no more texts or calls from the ghost-hunter.

"Ed Lockhart is missing?" said Desiree, her voice squeaky with panic. "We have to find him!"

"One thing at a time," said Wendy. "Let's do this reversal, so everyone can clear their heads, and then we can find your friend."

"We've got some weed in our room," said Joan. "Let's go."

"Maybe Ed's there," said Veronica as she stood up.

The whole gang trooped up to the seventh floor, Neo pausing to gather up all of his gadgets and spices, catching up with them again at the elevator.

Joan opened the door to their room, hoping to see Ed napping in his sleeping bag. The room was deserted, and she felt another pang of worry. Where could he be? Wendy obviously hadn't kidnapped him too — she'd been with them this whole time, and besides, she was on their side now and they had a truth spell to prove it.

Brandon brushed past her and grabbed one of the shopping bags from the dispensary, handing Wendy a jar of cannabis buds and a pipe.

"Excellent. This will do nicely," she said. With practiced hands, she packed a bud into the bowl.

"And now I suppose you need another drop of everyone's blood," sighed Joan.

"Just one of you should be fine. You said I used Brandon's to set it, right? So his would be best to remove it."

Brandon held out his arm and Wendy removed another finger stick from her purse, pricking his finger and dripping the blood onto the bud.

"Ew, are you going to smoke his blood?" said Desiree.

Wendy shrugged, lighter ready, poised to smoke. "You get used to doing all kinds of weird shit with blood as soon as you start practicing witchcraft."

"Don't you need him to be in the center of a pentagram made of weed?" asked Joan. "That's what you had set up in the office at the bar."

"Did I?" Wendy frowned and lowered the pipe. "Crap. I wish I could remember." She snapped her fingers. "Wait a moment. Didn't you say I was looking at a tablet?"

Wendy rummaged in her purse again and retrieved her tablet.

Joan peeked at the screen over her shoulder as she navigated into her notes app, scrolling past grocery lists and notes with such inscrutable titles as *The Orchid's Bloom* and *Seven Carrots and a Beet.*

"There!" Joan pointed. "*Hunkalicious!* That's got to be Brandon."

"Aw, thanks, babe." Brandon nudged her gently with his elbow.

"Don't call me that," said Joan absently, as Wendy clicked on the note.

"This is it!" said Wendy. "Good eye, Joan."

Joan's attention wandered as Wendy read through the note. She glanced at Brandon and saw he was looking at her, a small smile on his lips.

"What?" she asked, automatically smoothing down her hair.

He stepped toward her, wrapping an arm around her waist and planting a kiss on her forehead. "Nothing. You're pretty. And you think I'm hunky. It's nice."

She found herself grinning like an idiot. "Yeah. It is."

"Okay, I think I've got it," said Wendy at last. She strode over to the desk chair and moved it into an open space. Then she picked up the dispensary jar again and began arranging the rest of the buds in a rough pentagram. "I think this should do it. Brandon, you sit here."

Brandon took a seat.

"And now I'm going to light up, so my blood has a similar composition to Marian's when she cursed you." Wendy lit the pipe and inhaled deeply. That familiar sweet smoke filled the air.

Joan glanced toward the window, but it didn't look like it would open. Her card was so going to get charged extra for this.

She heard a whirring sound and glanced toward it to see Neo emerging from the bathroom. "I figured a fan couldn't hurt," he said.

Wendy ignored all of this, examining her tablet again. "Now I'm supposed to get into a similar mindset."

"What? Super-annoyed?" said Joan.

"Yeah, I guess. According to my notes, I thought it was anger. I'm sure being trapped in a pyramid of storage racks did that nicely. I wonder what I was doing before that to accomplish it."

"What usually makes you angry?" asked Veronica.

"Racism?" suggested Joan. "The ravages of modern capitalism? Those shoes with all the holes in them?"

"Crocs," supplied Brandon.

"Right." Of course, Brandon the shoe expert to the rescue.

"Crocs do annoy me," said Wendy. "And Uggs too."

"Knock-off Birkenstocks," suggested Brandon. "Like regular ones aren't ugly enough."

"Worn with fucking socks!" agreed Wendy. "Just why?"

"Are you annoyed now?" asked Finn.

"You're damn right I am! Just thinking about some idiot in cheap canvas sandals with purple socks, probably a broom skirt too—"

"What's next?" prompted Joan.

Wendy glared at her. "And I hate being interrupted. Oh, right." She glanced at the tablet again. "To re-curse you, I repeated the final words of the original. I guess I have to say the opposite. What's the opposite of a curse?"

"A blessing?" said Desiree.

"Fucking know-it-all linguist," muttered Wendy. She huffed and intoned, "And so I bless you – and I bless you – I bless you – bless you!"

Joan stiffened as an all-too-familiar jolt of electricity coursed through her body, leaving her shaken and weary a moment later. She closed her eyes, letting out all of her breath.

When she opened her eyes, she could see that Veronica and Brandon had gotten the same.

Joan staggered against Brandon's shoulder and lowered herself to the floor beside his chair, as Finn supported Veronica to a seat on the bed.

Desiree and Neo watched with wide eyes.

"Well? Did it work?" asked Wendy, drumming her fingernails impatiently on the desk.

"I think so," said Joan.

Her phone chirped and she pulled it from her purse, hands still shaky. "Sadie says they all felt it back home too."

Joan quickly typed out a text to let Sadie know the good news. The curse was gone. For now.

Epilogue

No sooner had Joan put away her phone when Ed burst into the room, frantically shouting, "Are you guys here? We gotta scram!"

He slid to a halt, taking in the scene with wide eyes. "What the hell is going on here?"

"Where have you been? What's going on?" demanded Veronica at the same time.

"There's no time!" Ed yelled. "Mrs. Olsen is here. And she saw me. And she's pissed! I think she just recursed me too."

He pointed at Wendy. "What is she doing here?"

"She's good now," said Joan. "We did a truth spell. You didn't get recursed – you got uncursed."

Ed shook his head, grabbing random items and tossing them into open suitcases. "There's no time!" he repeated. "Pack it all up! Let's go! Back home! Did you hear me?"

His panic was contagious, and Joan found herself frantically stuffing her bags with anything around that she could find, regardless of who it belonged to.

She dashed out the door, her suitcase careening onto one wheel as they all raced toward the car.

***

Author's Note:

Hi again! You've officially made it through **two books of the Rhymes With Witch series**, and I appreciate you so much for sticking with it!

Ready for more?

You can grab **Book 3** right here:

And if you pause here for now, thank you for reading. I hope to see you again soon.

Cheers,

Anna

ABOUT THE AUTHOR

Anna McCluskey is an Oregon-based, semi-nomadic, almost-entirely-feral fantasy author.

Anna is the author of the *Mathilda Holiday* series, the *Rhymes With Witch* series, the *Warrior Mage Librarians* series, and the upcoming stand-alone anthology *The Bloody Unicorn and Other Delightfully Dark Drinks*.

She has had several poems published in journals and anthologies, and her short fiction has been read by at least a dozen people, many of whom murmured appreciatively about it.

For information on upcoming projects and general merriment, check out her website, www.annamccluskey.com.

www.ingramcontent.com/pod-product-compliance
Lightning Source LLC
Chambersburg PA
CBHW050150110726
47898CB00008B/2741